PRAISE FOR
THE TEMPTATION SAGA

"Is it hot in here? Congratulations, Ms. Hardt. You dropped me into the middle of a scorching hot story and let me burn."
~ Seriously Reviewed

"I took this book to bed with me and I didn't sleep until 4 a.m. Yes, it's that damn engrossing, so grab your copy now!"
~Whirlwind Books

"Temptation never tasted so sweet... Both tempting, and a treasure... this book held many of the seductive vices I've come to expect from Ms. Hardt's work."
~Bare Naked Words

Taking

CATIE

THE TEMPTATION SAGA
BOOK THREE

WATERHOUSE PRESS

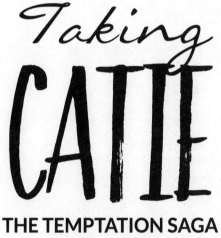

Taking CATIE

THE TEMPTATION SAGA
BOOK THREE

*To the men and women of the rodeo,
some of the greatest athletes in the world.*

CHAPTER ONE

Chad McCray loved women. Brunette, blond, or redhead, thin and willowy or curvy and voluptuous, he adored them all. Exploring their bodies and sating his sexual hunger was his favorite hobby.

Yes, he did adore women.

Commitment?

Not so much.

Since women seemed to love him as well, life had been good for his thirty-two years. In his two decades of loving the fairer sex, only one had tried badgering him into commitment. He'd gotten rid of her faster than a bucking bronc tosses a cowpoke. Now, he was on his way out the door to pick up a new luscious lollipop he'd met at a community potluck. Light blond hair, cherry-red lips, and curves that went on forever—Amber Cross, the new manicurist in town, was a tasty treat he looked forward to sampling.

The ring of his cell phone interrupted his lascivious thoughts. He scooped it out of his pocket and stared at the screen. His brother Zach.

"What's up, Zach?"

"Got an opportunity of a lifetime for you, Chad," Zach's deep voice said.

"What might that be?"

"Well, it seems you, Dallas, and I have been chosen to judge the rodeo queen contest this year."

Chad guffawed into the phone. "You mean Dusty and Annie are going to let you and Dallas ogle the cheesecake of Bakersville? You've got to be kidding." The mere thought of his disgustingly happily married brothers judging a beauty pageant brought a smirk to his lips. "I, on the other hand, would be honored."

Zach chuckled. "Our wives trust us. We're committed."

"Should *be* committed, you mean." Chad checked his watch. "Do you need anything else at the moment? I'm due to meet a lovely little cream puff in half an hour."

"Meet her? You mean you're not picking her up at her place?"

"Nope. We're meeting at the Bullfrog for a drink."

"One day, little brother," Zach said, "you're going to meet a woman who knocks your boots right off. A woman you want to treat like a lady."

"Not likely," Chad said. "My life is pretty darn perfect the way it is. When I need a home cooked meal, I crash your house or Dallas's. And when I want a critter fix, I have Sean and the twins. All the family love, but none of the responsibility. That's the way I like it."

"Sean's my critter, and the twins are Dallas's." Zach's tone turned serious. "Don't you want one of your own? You're not getting any younger, you know."

"Worried about my biological clock, Zach?" Chad laughed.

"Nope," his brother said. "Just worried you're going to wake up one day and find yourself alone."

Chad smiled, imagining the sweet red lips of Miss Amber Cross roaming over every inch of his body. "One thing I can guarantee you, brother. I'll never be alone."

★ ★ ★

Caitlyn Bay ran into her brother's arms at baggage claim in Denver. Fatigued and dehydrated from the trip from Paris, she looked a mess.

"Hey, Catie-bug," Harper said, kissing the top of her head. He pushed her away. "Let me look at you. You're all grown up."

"You just saw me in Brussels at Christmas, Harper," Catie said, "and right now I'm a fright."

"Nonsense, you're gorgeous as always. People at home aren't even going to recognize you. You left four years ago a freckle-faced girl in ponytails, and now you're a chic Parisian grad student." He shook his head. "I still don't know why you never came home for the holidays." He steadied her as she stumbled. "And still a notorious klutz."

Catie ignored the jibe. "You know why. I wanted to travel, to see the world. And I did, Harp. I saw it all."

"I think you stayed away to avoid a certain cowboy by the name of McCray," Harper said. "Chad's still single, you know."

Catie looked away. "My bags here yet?"

"Your plane just got in, honey. Your bags'll be a few minutes. Nice save, by the way."

"What do you mean?" she asked innocently. Inside, her heart was thumping like the hooves of a racehorse at the thought of Chad McCray.

"He's damn near twice your age, Catie."

"I have no interest in Chad McCray. And he hasn't been twice my age since I was eleven and he was twenty-two. Even so, I happen to be twenty-one years old now, as you well know. Legal and everything. I can even order a margarita when I want one. In fact, I think I want one now."

"Now?"

"Heck, yeah. I'm exhausted, and my brain is fried. I can't think of a better salve for myself at the moment. Mind if we stop at the Bullfrog on the way home?"

"I think you've lost your mind, little sis. You've never set foot in the Bullfrog."

"Because I haven't been able to. Legally. But now I can. I want my big brother to buy me my first legal drink."

"You've been drinking in France for four years."

Catie gave her brother a friendly swat. "You make it sound like I'm some kind of a lush. You know I hardly ever indulge. But right now a little lime and tequila sounds thirst-quenching good. You can't get a Colorado margarita in Paris, Harp."

"Even with all that Grand Marnier and Cointreau they got there?" Harper's handsome face twisted into a teasing grin.

"Give me plain old Triple Sec and Cuervo any day," Catie said. "And I can't wait to sink my teeth into some Colorado Angus. French food is wonderful, but I sure have missed Colorado cuisine."

"Ma's got a big homecoming planned at the house tomorrow night," Harper said. "Everyone shy of Murphy'll be there"—he winked—"including Chad McCray."

"I couldn't give two puny figs," Catie said, avoiding her brother's gaze.

Her words came out strong, with a huff and a scorn.

But they were one big ol' lie.

★ ★ ★

The Bullfrog Lounge featured live music and the best

margaritas outside of Mexico. Or so the sign said. Mostly what the bar featured was a crowded dance floor that forced couples to mesh together whether the music was fast or slow. This suited Chad just fine. Miss Amber Cross was as gorgeous as he remembered, and tonight a tight denim skirt hugged those narrow hips like a snakeskin. Her bodacious breasts nearly poured out of her snug cotton tank top, and her platinum waves settled nicely over her sleek golden shoulders. Lips as red and full as he remembered, and he'd already had the pleasure of sampling them while they sat at the bar sipping their drinks. Another drink, a few more close dances, and he figured she'd be ready to hit the sack.

"What are you thinking about, cowboy?" Amber asked, as Chad led her back to their seats at the bar.

"Thinking another drink might be in order, honey."

Amber sat down on her bar stool and crossed her creamy thighs. "That dancing did make me thirsty."

"What'll it be this time?"

"Same thing. A cosmo, I think."

Chad chuckled under his breath. Those girly drinks did nothing for him. His brothers favored scotch and bourbon, but Chad was a beer man all the way. "One cosmo for the lady," he told the bartender, "and another Fat Tire for me." Chad threw a twenty on the counter. "Keep the change."

"So tell me more about the infamous McCray brothers," Amber said. "I've heard lots, but being new here, I'm not sure what's gossip and innuendo and what's truth."

Chad let out a boisterous laugh. "Honey, it's all gossip here in Bakersville. It's a small town, and everybody knows everybody else's business. What exactly have you heard?"

"Just that you all are the richest men in town, owners of

the largest ranch. And you all love the ladies." Her sweet lips curved in to a flirtatious grin.

"Honey, my big brothers are both married. Lovesick as they come."

"Oh? Are they as fine looking as you are, Chad?"

"Some say finer." Chad winked. "Dallas, he's the oldest, is married to Annie, the vet here in town. They have twin girls, Sylvie and Laurie, named after their grandmas. And Zach, he's the middle brother, is married to a sweet little girl we've known since we were kids. He and Dusty have a four-year-old boy, Sean."

"And your parents? They still around?"

"My pa died nearly ten years ago and my ma just last year."

"Goodness. I'm sorry. I didn't mean to bring up bad memories."

"It's okay, honey. My ma had aggressive breast cancer. By the time she was diagnosed, the docs only gave her a year to live. She made it two. We consider that good fortune."

"Wow." Amber took a sip of the cocktail the bartender set in front of her. "I'm real sorry. That's tough."

"It was, but we're fine. We're muddling through. My brothers have their families, and they take good care of me."

"Meaning?"

"Meaning, I can crash with them when I need some family time. Mostly I hang at my own place, though. And speaking of my place"—he took her hand and rubbed his calloused thumb over her smooth manicured fingers—"I've got the makings for more cosmos there. And the sweetest black lab you'd ever want to meet."

"Oh, I love dogs," Amber gushed.

"Marnie'd love to meet you, honey," he said, circling his thumb in her palm. A little hand massage always sent the right message.

"You have remarkable hands," Amber said, closing her eyes. "Ever think of going into the nail business?" She let out a girlish giggle.

"Can't say I have, honey," Chad said. "My ranch keeps me pretty darn busy."

"Mmm. Well, you sure know how to give a good hand massage. Come by the shop sometime, and I'll return the favor. No charge."

"I've got a better idea." He dropped her hand and ran his fingers up the smooth silk or her arms and shoulders.

"What's that?"

"How about you give me that massage tonight?" He leaned over and kissed her lips lightly. "At my place."

"You are just one sweet-talking cowboy, aren't you, Chad McCray?"

"Is that a yes?"

"What must you think of me? Barely in town a month and going home with a man I hardly know."

"I think we're attracted to each other. What's wrong with that? As for barely knowing me—" He trailed his lips to her ear and nipped her lobe. "I guarantee you by morning we'll know each other a whole heckuva lot better."

She shuddered under his mouth, and he smiled against her cheek. Bingo.

"Sure, it sounds fun," Amber said. "Let's go."

Chad chugged the last of his beer, took Amber's hand to lead her to the door of the bar, and ran smack dab into his neighbor Harper Bay.

"Watch where you're going, Bay," he said jovially. "You damn near knocked me off my feet."

"Hey, Chad," Harper said, "who do you have there?"

"This is Amber. She's working for Judy at the beauty shop. Amber, Harper Bay. He runs the ranch next to ours."

"Nice to meet you."

"A pleasure," Harper said, taking Amber's hand. "Can you hold on a minute, there's someone I know would like to see you."

"Who?"

"Give her a minute," Harper said. "She went to freshen up."

"Her?" Chad's brain churned. Who would Harper have with him? He looked toward the ladies room, and within ten seconds, a goddess emerged. Tall and sleek, with mahogany hair that drifted past her shoulders in silky waves and a face that could rival Helen of Troy in beauty. And a body...breasts as luscious as any, curvy hips, and long legs that went on forever in those clingy jeans. Who the hell was she?

Harper turned and grabbed the woman's hand. "You remember Catie, don't you, Chad?"

Chad's stomach dropped, as did his jaw. This was Catie Bay? Little Catie Bay, who used to wear her brown hair in pigtails and spent her life in the barn with her horses?

Had she always had breasts?

Where were the freckles? The braids? The...little girl? Where was the damn little girl? That little girl had nursed a mega-crush on Chad growing up. He and his brothers had always known. Ever since he'd been paired up with Catie's older sister, Angelina, for a project in high school and he'd spent massive time at the Bay ranch. Catie'd been four then and had followed Chad around like a lovesick pup. Damn, she'd been a cute little thing. He'd seen her a lot over the years, watched her grow up. Hell, he'd danced with her at Dallas's wedding. She wasn't more than seventeen at the time, and he'd been, what? Twenty-eight or so? She'd been turning into a pretty thing then, but she was still a kid.

Then another image flashed through Chad's mind—the last time he'd seen Catie Bay. At her eighteenth birthday party, some four years ago now. She'd cornered him in the private gazebo at her ranch, and...

His groin tightened.

He was eleven years her senior, and he'd stopped it. But it had been damn near the hardest thing he'd ever done. He remembered luscious eighteen-year-old lips clambering to touch his. Perky eighteen-year-old nipples poking through her silky green dress. Damn, she'd looked good in green, but she was a kid. Still had a light spray of freckles across her nose...

This woman standing next to Harper was no kid.

Nope, no kid at all.

CHAPTER TWO

Catie inhaled, closed her eyes, and hoped beyond hope the ground might open up beneath her and swallow her whole. What in the hell had Harper been thinking? She'd seen herself in the mirror in the restroom. The ten hour flight hadn't been kind. Her hair was limp, her eyes puffy, and her left cheek still had a faint imprint from the airplane seat where she'd fallen asleep for a blessed two hours. Still, she was shy about six more hours of slumber, and her face and body showed it. Thankfully, she hadn't tripped coming out of the bathroom.

Chad McCray.

He was still the most handsome man she'd ever seen. His dark walnut hair fell to his shoulders in silky waves—silky waves she'd fantasized running her fingers through more than once. His brown eyes were long lashed and mesmerizing, and now, little crinkly laugh lines added to their allure. His sinewy and sexy forearms were as muscular as ever, and those wispy brown hairs still peeked out from his western shirt. Tall, the tallest of the McCray boys at six-feet-four—the most beautiful cowboy she'd ever laid eyes on.

And clinging to him was a pretty blond woman. A jolt of jealousy hit Catie in the gut.

Had she really wanted to come to the Bullfrog? What had she been thinking? Her margarita could wait.

Too late now, though.

"Hi, Chad," she said, and held out her hand. Might as well

make the best of the situation. She was an adult now, not some drooling kid with a crush. So she didn't look her best. She could still act the part.

"Catie, I can't believe it," Chad said. "I wouldn't have recognized you. You've sure grown up. Where the heck have you been? Why didn't you come home to visit more often?"

"Well, I—"

"She hasn't been home at all," Harper said. "She's been traveling the world with her global friends." He laughed. "But I hope we can convince her to stay for a while, now that she's here."

"Uh, Chad?" The pretty blond woman tugged at his sleeve.

"Oh, I'm sorry. Catie, this is Amber. Amber, Catie."

"Caitlyn," Catie said. "I go by Caitlyn now."

"It's nice to meet you, Caitlyn," Amber said. "I just moved here from San Antonio."

"Really? How nice," Catie said. "Would the two of you care to join us for a drink? I told Harper I just had to have a Colorado margarita after that plane ride. You must excuse me, I know I'm a mess. Overseas flights are a killer." Catie stopped to take a breath. She was talking too fast. And what was she thinking? Inviting them for a drink. Chad McCray was the last cowboy in Bakersville she wanted to have a drink with.

Yeah, right.

"Yeah, please join us," Harper said. "The more, the merrier."

"We were just leaving," Amber said, "but I'd love a rain check. How about it, Chad?"

"You don't mind if we join them, do you?"

Chad's words were for Amber, but he raked his gaze over

Catie. Her heart sank. She didn't want him to see her like this. He was no doubt thinking she looked as bad as she felt.

"Well..." Amber fidgeted with her small purse.

"You're new here, honey," he said, and the word "honey" sent another slice into Catie's gut. "Don't you want to meet more people?"

"Of course I do." Amber continued to fidget.

Catie felt a little sorry for her. She seemed like a perfectly nice person, and Chad had totally put her on the spot. Of course, she was Chad's date for the evening, so Catie didn't feel all that bad.

Then again, Chad always had a date.

Ever since that fifteen-year-old boy had strutted into her house to work with Angie on some sociology project, he'd been a ladies' man. He'd never dated Angie, but he'd dated every other pretty thing in Bakersville. Every time he had, another chisel had chipped away at Catie's heart.

Her little girl crush had never gone away. She'd always thought it would, had actually hoped it would, but nope, it'd only gotten stronger over the years. When she hit puberty herself at twelve, it turned into full blown heart-breaking puppy love. Puppy love that bloomed and grew for the next six years.

Deciding to attend the Sorbonne in Paris had been Catie's own idea. Her mother had balked at it, saying the distance was too far to go for college, but Catie had wanted to leave Bakersville. Leave the whole U.S.A. She loved her country, but she thought if she got away from Chad McCray, maybe she could stop pining over him.

She'd left after her eighteenth birthday, though she'd made the decision several months earlier. On her eighteenth birthday, though, after her botched seduction attempt with Chad, she'd realized the decision had been a good one. A perfect one. She needed to get over Chad McCray.

That's why she hadn't come home for four years.

Oh, the traveling had been fun, and she'd learned and experienced so much. Wonderful memories and amazing friendships that she'd treasure forever.

But the traveling wasn't why she hadn't returned.

The reason she'd stayed away was embodied in the tall and ruggedly handsome cowboy staring at her.

"Well, then," she said, trying her darnedest to act nonchalant, "let's have a seat, shall we? I'm thirsting for that Colorado margarita."

She took Amber's arm, bypassing Chad. "It's wonderful to meet you. What brought you to Bakersville?"

"I'm working for Judy at the salon. I do nails."

"Oh, how nice." Catie led Amber to a table for four in a corner. "Mine are a fright. I'll have to come see you."

"Oh, yes, please do. I'm just starting to build my clientele." Amber sat down next to Chad and possessively glommed onto his arm. "I'd appreciate any new business."

"I imagine I'll be coming in for the works in a few days," Catie said. "Traveling does terrible things to my hair." She shook her head and tried to act casual. "I need a facial, too."

"Sheesh, Catie, what's all this girl talk?" Harper said. "Let's get you that margarita. Then you can tell us about your trip to Greece."

"Greece?" Chad shook his head. "You went to Greece, little bit?"

Little bit? Chad McCray hadn't changed. She tried to ignore the nickname. "Yes, my friend Dominic and I spent two weeks there during spring break. It's gorgeous, as you can imagine."

"She'll have all her photos at the shindig tomorrow night," Harper said. "You're coming aren't you, Chad?"

"Sure, wouldn't miss it," Chad said, his gaze meeting Catie's. Again.

Amber looked self-conscious, biting her lip. Should Catie invite her? Would Chad? She waited a moment, but Chad said nothing.

Catie turned to Amber. "I hope you can come. It'd be a chance to meet lots of folks. My silly mama thinks everyone in town wants to hear all about my travels." She smiled as Amber started to relax. "But it's really just an excuse for a big party. Please say you'll come."

"I'd love to come," Amber said. "Thank you for the invitation. I'll need to get directions to your place."

"Chad can pick you up, can't you?" Harper said.

"Uh, sure. Yeah, I can do that." Chad played with the collar of his shirt. "You working tomorrow?"

"Till six," Amber said.

"I'll pick you up at Judy's at six, then. Will that work?"

"Sure, that'd be fine."

A waitress interrupted their conversation and took their drink orders. Chad and Harper started talking about ranching, seeming to forget all about her trip to Greece. Amber smiled up at Chad, her hand resting possessively on his arm.

When Catie's margarita came, she took a long drink. The salt around the rim stung her lips, chapped from the dry air on the plane.

Nothing like it.

She chugged the rest and stood up, her head a bit hazy.

When had she last eaten? On the plane sometime.

"I want to dance," she announced, and grabbed her handsome cowboy's arm. "Come on, Chad."

"Little bit," Chad said, as she dragged him away, "are you sure you want to do this?"

"Sure I'm sure," Catie said. "It's just a dance."

"You drank that 'rita awful fast, sugar."

Sugar? She liked the sound of that. "A little tequila, a little Garth Brooks, a little dance with a handsome cowboy. Sounds like heaven."

"Whatever you say, little bit."

"Little bit?" She looked into his eyes, so dark they were nearly black. They seemed to smoke. "I like sugar better."

"Okay," he drawled. "Come on." He snaked his arms around her waist. "Let's cut the rug, sugar."

The song wasn't made for slow dancing, but the crowd on the dance floor necessitated closeness between them. Chad's hard body crushed against her, and her pulse quickened.

"I'm glad you decided not to ignore me all night."

"Ignore you?"

"Yeah, you talking on and on with Amber, when it's clear to a saint you and she have nothin' at all in common." He chuckled. "You sure have changed, little...I mean, sugar," Chad said. "I hardly recognized you."

"It's been four years, Chad."

"What happened to the little girl who loved horses more than people?"

"She's still in here."

"I admit, I sure was surprised you left your mare. You must have had a huge reason for leaving the country."

"Oh, I did."

"What was it?"

"Maybe I'll tell you sometime," she said coyly.

"Okay, sugar." He chuckled. "I'll hold you to that."

The music changed from fast to slow, and she leaned into Chad's muscles, closed her eyes, and inhaled. Leather. Leather and cinnamon. And Chad. Musky, male, perfect Chad. If anything, he'd become even more appealing in the four years she'd been gone.

They swayed gently to the music, their bodies melting together in all the right places. Catie slipped into a dreamworld, a world she hadn't dared visit in the last four years. A world she'd thought she could forget.

No. She couldn't forget. They might have only this one dance, but she'd make it worthwhile. She pulled away just a smidge and stared up into Chad's face. She wanted only to look at him, to drink him in. But his dark eyes smoldered, and she read something in them. Something she couldn't quite decipher.

"Sugar?" His voice cracked. Just a little, but she noticed.

"Hmm?"

He shook his head slightly. "Goddamn, sugar."

He lowered his mouth to hers.

CHAPTER THREE

They were the softest, sweetest lips Chad McCray had ever kissed, and he'd kissed a lot. Laced with lime and a touch of salt from her margarita, but mostly they tasted of sweet raspberry wine. Who would have known Catie Bay tasted so good?

Catie Bay.

Little Catie Bay.

Little bit.

Damn.

Chad ripped his lips from hers. Thank God he hadn't sunk his tongue into her mouth. He'd have been lost then. This way, it remained a friendly kiss. A welcome home kiss. Nothing special, just a little peck between friends.

Damn, he wanted more. He wanted to taste the sweet secrets of her mouth, of that beautiful body pressed against him. Her pert little nipples were hard berries protruding through her cotton blouse. They jutted out, begging for his attention. Had any man had tasted them before? His groin tightened, and he wished, if only for a second, that he could be the first to suck them into hard little pebbles. The first to run his tongue over the silky contours of her body, to taste the nectar she had to offer.

Get hold of yourself, McCray. This is little Catie Bay!

Little Catie Bay who was still looking into his eyes with lusty desire. Hell, she had no idea what she was doing to him.

"Come on, sugar," he said, "let's get back to the table."

"I wanna dance."

"Another time." He led her back, his fingers entwining with hers of their own volition. Why did her hand feel so good in his?

Amber was deep in conversation with Harper. Thank God she hadn't seen him kiss Catie. But he had invited her home with him.

Strange thing, he was no longer interested in a roll in the hay with Amber.

Right now, he wanted a roll in the hay with one sugar-lipped Caitlyn Bay.

He was definitely headed for hell in a hand basket.

"Having fun?" he asked Amber, when he and Catie returned to the table.

"Oh, yeah. Harper's a barrel of laughs." Amber giggled. "But don't you think we should be going, Chad? I do have to work tomorrow."

"Okay. Sure, we can go." He held out his hand to Amber, trying to come up with a way to get out of taking her home with him. They left the bar and he walked her to her car.

"Honey," he said, "I'm going to have to take a rain check on that hand massage. I just remembered I have an early day tomorrow. Promised my brothers I'd help them with a few projects. You don't mind, do you?"

"Oh." Amber's face fell.

Chad felt like a heel. She was nice enough girl, but he was no longer interested. What the hell was the matter with him? Pretty face and a hot body, and all he could think about was getting into Catie Bay's pants. He was hell-bound for sure. Maybe a night in Amber's bed was exactly what he needed.

"You know, maybe it'd be okay after all," Chad said. "If

you took your own car. I..." Okay, this was awkward. "I have to get up real early, so you wouldn't be able to spend the night."

"I think I get what you're saying," Amber said. "I'll take that rain check. I have an early day tomorrow too. And don't worry about Harper's party tomorrow night. I can find my own way."

"Now come on, honey, don't be like that. This is just a little bump in the road. I can take you to the Bay shindig."

"Well..."

"I don't mind at all. I'll pick you up at the salon at six like we planned, okay?"

Amber smiled. She sure was pretty. So why wasn't his libido on fire? Didn't make any sense at all.

"Okay. I'd like that. See you tomorrow, then."

Chad closed the car door for her and watched as she drove off. He walked back toward the entrance to the bar, and out came a whiff of roses and raspberries. Catie.

"Hey," he said. "You all right?"

"Yeah, I'm fine. Just needed some air." She laughed, a little shakily. "Shouldn't have had that second margarita."

"When's the last time you ate? Or slept?"

"I slept and ate on the plane."

"You're all jet-lagged, sugar. You'd best get home and get to bed. No more 'ritas for you until you've had a decent night's sleep and a decent meal."

"Now you sound just like Harper," Catie said. "I happen to be twenty-one, for your information. I'm certainly capable of taking care of myself."

"Twenty-one." Chad chuckled. Twenty-one had been so long ago. "You're just a baby. Let's get you back inside, and Harper can take you home."

"I am not a baby, Chad McCray." She stomped her foot adamantly, barely missing Chad's boot-clad toe. "I haven't been a baby for a very long time. You just never took notice."

"Well, you haven't exactly been around for me to take notice," Chad said. Why was he engaging in this infantile conversation? What the heck did he care? "Come with me, sugar."

"I will not."

"Oh, yes, you will." He grabbed her arm, shocked at the tingles he felt when he touched her.

She jerked her arm away. "I'm not a baby, you stupid cowboy, and I'll prove it."

She clamped her arms around his neck and pulled his face to hers. Her lips claimed his in a forceful open-mouthed kiss. Lime again, and raspberries. Sweet, soft lips. Chad couldn't help himself. His tongue met hers and tangled, devouring the hidden treasures of her mouth.

He nibbled at her lips, her tongue, and then moved to her cheek, raining tender kisses along her jawline, up to her ear.

"God, you taste good, sugar," he whispered.

Her sigh was sweet as spring rain against his neck. "Kiss me again, Chad. Please."

She didn't have to ask twice. He crushed his mouth to hers and drank of her intoxicating sweetness. Where had she learned to kiss like a little siren? Her tongue inched along his lips, his teeth. When she sucked the point of his tongue into her mouth, his groin tightened and pulsed inside his jeans. He grabbed her and rubbed his arousal against her. That body. That luscious, tempting body.

But this was Catie Bay.

Little Catie Bay.

What the hell am I doing?

He broke the suction of the kiss with a loud smack. "Sugar. We can't do this."

"Why not? We're both adults."

"No." He stopped to catch his breath, which was coming in rapid puffs. Damn, he wanted her. Wanted to sink into her softness with every part of his body. Especially one particularly persistent part.

"Chad—"

"Come on." He led her back into the Bullfrog. "Harper needs to get you home. You need sleep. Or maybe you should eat first. Aw crap, I don't know, but you need to get the hell out of here."

"Why?"

"Because if you don't, something's gonna happen that we'll both regret come morning."

"I'd never regret it, Chad."

"Yeah, sugar, you would. Trust me."

"Don't tell me what I'd regret and what I wouldn't, Chad McCray." She stomped her foot again and looked charmingly indignant with her hands on her luscious hips. "I've been in Europe for four years. Europe, where nude beaches are the rage and indiscriminate sex is as common as a—"

Chad clamped his hand over Catie's mouth. "Christ, sugar, shut up, will you? You're just a babe. You can't lie on a nude beach. As for sex... I hope to hell you don't know what you're talking about."

"Mmmffpph," she said under his hand.

"I'm taking you back into Harper, and you're going home. You and I are going to forget this mistake of a kiss ever happened."

Catie stopped struggling—why? Chad didn't know—and let him take her back to Harper. Once she and Harper were safely on their way home, he found his pickup and started the engine. He inhaled sharply, trying to get his bearings. A slight aroma of raspberries wafted to his nose. Catie. Her scent still lingered on his clothes, her sweet taste on his lips.

He hoped to God she could forget their kiss, but one thing was for damn sure.

He never would.

★ ★ ★

Maria Bay crushed Catie into her arms. "Home, finally. Where have you two been, Harp?"

"Catie wanted to stop at the Bullfrog."

"The Bullfrog? Land sakes."

"I just wanted a margarita, Mama," Catie said. "The plane ride was harrowing. And then there was the two-hour drive to Bakersville."

"I could have made you a perfectly fine margarita here," her mother said, "though God knows why it couldn't have waited. I'm so glad you're finally home."

"Just push me toward my room," Catie said. "I need to fall into bed."

"I understand completely, sweetie, but Angie's on her way over, and I thought we'd have a nice late supper together."

"Ma, Catie's been up for twenty-four hours," Harper said.

"I slept a little on the plane." Catie's mouth cracked open in a wide yawn.

"Well, well, little Catie-bug." Catie's father, Wayne Bay, entered the room, big as a bear and just as cuddly.

"Daddy!" Catie ran into his arms.

"Let me look at you, sweetheart."

"You just saw me at Christmas, Daddy."

"True enough, but let me look at you back in your own home. It's sure been lonely around here the past four years. Did you see Ladybird?"

"Of course. Harp and I stopped at the corral before we came up to the house. I had to see my precious. You've taken great care of her, Daddy."

"Thank the hands, darlin'. They knew you'd be back eventually and you'd check her out real good. Feel up to a ride?"

Catie yawned again. "I can't believe I'm going to say this, but not tonight. I need to get to bed. I'm absolutely exhausted."

"What about Mama's dinner? And Angie?"

"All right, all right. Can I just lie down a minute? Why don't you all come get me when Angie shows up?"

"Sounds fair to me," her father said, grabbing one of the suitcases Harper had set in the foyer. "Harper and I'll bring up your luggage. The rest of your stuff arrived yesterday."

"Good," Catie said. "I'll see you all in a little while."

She trudged up the stairs to her room and flopped on her canopy bed, all pink and ruffled. Yuck. Had she really been the girl who lived in this room? Horse posters everywhere. Tomorrow she'd think about redecorating. But tonight...

She yawned again, her lungs expanding. Closing her eyes, she remembered soft, full masculine lips traveling up her jawline to her earlobe.

Mmm. Chad McCray. She slipped into a dream.

CHAPTER FOUR

Catie's family had taken pity on her and let her sleep through the night, even after Angie had shown up. The next morning, she showered and dressed. After a delicious Colorado breakfast of a Denver omelet made with fresh eggs gathered that morning and a thin cut Angus steak from the Bay Ranch on the western slope, Catie took Ladybird on a long ride, recapturing the beauty of her family's property in Bakersville. How had she stayed away so long? She and Ladybird got reacquainted, and within a half hour, they were riding as though she'd never left. She moved fluidly with her mare, galloping over the hilly knolls of her family's property. After two hours, she found herself at the border of McCray Landing, Chad's property, which he owned jointly with his brothers, Zach and Dallas. McCray Landing was the biggest and most successful beef ranch in Colorado. Bay Crossing, on the western slope, wasn't as big, but Catie's family also owned this property outside Bakersville which they called Cha Cha Ranch—for Caitlyn, Harper, and Angelina. Cha Cha—God, she hated that name— was small potatoes compared to McCray Landing. It had been gifted to Maria by a distant uncle when Catie was a toddler. The family had decided to make the move because there were better chances for good schooling for the Bay kids near the big city of Denver. Hands now ran Bay Crossing, and Wayne and Harper traveled to the western slope several times a year to keep up with things. Angie and Harper—at eleven and nine years older than Catie, respectively—remembered living on the western slope, but to Catie, Cha Cha was home and always would be.

The vastness of McCray landing still amazed Catie. Here she was, standing on the border, and she saw no cattle, no houses, no nothing. The ranch was that big. Dallas, Zach, and Chad all had their own places, though Dallas and his family had moved into the big ranch house when Laurie McCray had passed on a year ago. A tear trickled down Catie's cheek. Best friends with Catie's own mother, Laurie had been one of Catie's idols growing up.

She sniffed. She should have come home for Laurie's funeral. Maria had told her Laurie would understand how busy she was, but an anvil of guilt settled in Catie's stomach as she looked upon the land that had once been Laurie's.

She should have been here.

For Laurie, and for her own mother, who had lost her best friend.

And for Chad.

As the baby of the McCray boys, he had been very close to his mother.

But would he have wanted her here?

Tears fell again, for a different reason this time. For the kiss Chad had told her to forget.

She'd try like hell, she would, but she knew right now she'd never forget the intoxication of that meeting of mouths.

"Come on, Ladybird." Catie hugged the mare with her thighs, urging her into a trot. "Let's get back. I have a party to get ready for."

She'd look her best tonight. Not like some reincarnated dishrag who'd just spent over ten hours on a plane and two more hours in Harper's truck. Tonight, Chad would notice her again. She was determined to get another kiss, even if he wanted to forget the first one.

* * *

Catie had brushed her clean and soft hair until it shone and applied just a touch of blush and reddish lipstick. She never used mascara. Her black eyelashes were long and thick. But today she made an exception. She wanted to knock Chad McCray's Stetson off his head, and she couldn't help but notice that Amber had painted the stuff on last night. Maybe Chad liked that.

Her nails she kept clipped short, nothing like Amber's long red acrylics. Was that what Chad liked? Well, she'd find out, and if so, maybe she'd pay Miss Amber a visit.

Then again, taking care of Ladybird and her other ranch duties wouldn't allow for long fake nails. Chad would just have to take her as she was.

She donned a red sheath sundress that showed lots of thigh and red sandals with three-inch heels. Took her from five-nine to six-feet, but Chad was six-feet-four. Wouldn't matter an iota. Catie had grown comfortable with her height in Europe. She'd been mistaken for a model more than once. She smiled. Freckle-faced Catie-bug Bay, mistaken for a model. Did her heart—and her ego—good.

Guests had begun arriving a half hour ago, but Catie wasn't in a rush. She'd make an entrance, truth to tell. If only she knew whether Chad had arrived yet.

She sighed. It'd be rude to keep her guests any longer. After all, her mother had planned this shindig as a welcome home for her. She bit her lips to plump them, ran the brush through her dark waves once more, and left the security of her bedroom.

She walked down the stairs, her heart thumping at the thought of seeing Chad. Of kissing him again. She ambled through the sprawling ranch house to the patio doors, where friends and neighbors were milling about in the giant backyard. She noticed the oldest McCray, Dallas, and his wife, Annie, with two little toddlers who must be their twins, Laurie and Sylvie. Something else she'd missed. The birth of Chad's nieces. Why on earth had she stayed away?

"Catie, my God!" Annie McCray said, her New Jersey accent as pronounced as ever. "You look gorgeous, hon."

"Speak for yourself," Catie said, smiling. She liked Annie. And Annie was the picture of gorgeous. Long black hair that fell in ringlets and violet-blue eyes. Dressed in her signature peasant skirt and blouse, she could have walked right out of a gypsy harem. "It's so good to see you." She gave Annie a quick but firm hug. "This must be one of your twins."

"Yep." Annie picked up the pretty little girl at her feet and balanced her on her hip. "This is Sylvie."

"She's beautiful, Annie."

"She looks just like Dallas," Annie said. "The other one's more of a Dallas-Annie combo, but they both really look more like their pop. Dallas!" She waved him over. "Bring Laurie over here to see Catie."

"Oh, I don't know," Catie said, admiring the pretty child. "I see a lot of you in her. Look at all that hair."

The child's hair fell in dark ringlets, like Annie's, but her black eyes were all McCray.

"It's not as curly as mine, thank God," Annie said. "That's

what Dallas's hair would look like if he grew it longer."

Dallas walked over, holding the other twin. He was as ruggedly handsome as ever, his black hair reaching his collar, the gray at his temples strangely appealing. Several days' growth of beard covered his jawline. "Hey, little bit," he drawled, "sure is good to see you home."

"Good to see you, too," Catie said. "So this is little Laurie?"

"Yeah, this is ma's namesake. She's a beauty, isn't she? Like her mama."

Annie rolled her eyes. "I already told her they're both dead ringers for you."

"Nah. Laurie, here, she has Annie's cute little nose." Dallas smiled, his eyes crinkling.

Annie laughed, loud and boisterous, like the Jersey girl she was. "They both have your hair and your eyes."

"I'd've loved them to have Annie's pretty eyes," Dallas said. "But heck, we're not done yet, honey." He winked at his wife.

Catie should have been embarrassed by the innuendo, but Annie was so open and fun, there was no reason to be. She laughed as Dallas took Sylvie from Annie's arms and led the two girls inside the house to get them a drink.

"They're both beautiful," Catie said, and they were. Beautiful little McCray girls. A sigh, louder than she wanted, escaped her throat. What she would give to bear the next McCray baby.

As if she'd read Catie's mind, Annie said, "Chad's here, hon."

"Is he?"

Annie had always known about Catie's crush, and she was the only person in whom Catie had confided about it.

"But he came with the new manicurist in town, Amber something."

Annie put her hand on Catie's forearm—a gentle, comforting gesture, but it embarrassed Catie. She shrugged away.

"Why should I care who he's dating? I've been gone four years."

"I know. I know," Annie said. "But I also noticed how you've been searching this party since you and I started talking. I just assumed—"

"Oh, Annie." Catie sighed. "I saw him last night. Harp and I stopped off at the Bullfrog for a drink. He was with Amber then."

"So you know."

"Yeah. And I'm fine, really. That crush on Chad was a long time ago."

"He's still single, and no closer to commitment than he was four years ago when you left," Annie said. "Dallas and Zach give him crap about it, but he's bound and determined not to get serious. So if that's any consolation, I doubt he'll ever get serious about that blond powder puff."

Catie let out a giggle. Annie always made her feel better. "I was thinking the same thing. I mean, she's pretty and all, but that hair color has got to be fake."

"Straight out of a bottle, I'd bet," Annie agreed.

"And the nails... Of course, that's her job," Catie said.

"Fake as they come," Annie said, "and certainly not suited to life here in Bakersville. She'll find that out soon enough."

"So what's Chad doing?"

"He's playing the field, like he always does. Amber's new in town. Trust me, that's her only appeal. He'll grow tired of her. I've seen it time and time again."

"Yeah, yeah." Catie shrugged and let out a breathy sigh. "So I have I."

"How about the rodeo queen thing? Can you imagine?"

"What are you talking about?"

"Dallas, Zach, and Chad have been tapped to judge it this year."

"Really?" Catie's heart lurched. "When is it?"

"Next week, I think. I could check for you. Hey, you should enter."

Catie'd been thinking the same thing. After all, she'd been mistaken for a supermodel more than once in Europe. But rodeo queen? Was she too old?

"Do you know the requirements for the contest, Annie?"

"Heck no. But Dallas might, since he's judging. When he comes back, ask him."

"I will do just that," Catie said.

When Dallas returned with the twins, she pounced on him. "Tell me all about the rodeo queen competition, Dallas. Just what are the qualifications?"

"Heck, it's nothin' but the tarts of Bakersville struttin' their stuff, little bit. You don't want any part of it. You're way better than that."

Annie clicked her tongue. "Don't give her that, Dallas. She's genuinely interested. Look at her. She's gorgeous. She just might take the thing."

"Oh, I have no doubt of that." Dallas smiled. "That's not what I mean. You're too classy for a beauty pageant."

"But think of the good I could accomplish," Catie said, searching for something halfway intelligent to say. "I could do charitable work, and..."

"This ain't Miss America." Dallas guffawed. "It's the Bakersville Rodeo Queen."

"Good God, Cowboy, quit giving the girl crap and tell her the rules." Annie took one of the twins from Dallas.

"All right, all right, Doc. Simmer down." He turned to Catie. "It's for single ladies between the ages of eighteen and twenty-two."

"Good. I qualify."

"Sure you do," Dallas said. "And you're mighty pretty. As pretty as any woman around. But do you really want to strut around in a bikini in front of a bunch of lecherous old judges?" He grinned.

Catie laughed. "You and your brothers are the judges."

Annie swatted him, but Dallas kept grinning. "Need I say more?"

"Ha-ha," Catie said. "Where do I sign up?"

"It's pretty late, little bit. But I can probably get you in. I know the judges." He winked. "If you're sure."

"I'm sure, Dallas. As sure as anything. Thanks."

"All right, consider yourself entered."

Annie smiled and winked at Catie, and Catie curved her own lips upward in what she hoped was a saucy grin.

"I'll help you prepare, hon. We'll get Dusty, too. And no doubt your big sister has a few tricks up her sleeve. By the time we're done with you, you'll be the belle of Bakersville."

★ ★ ★

Amber's honeyed gaze was getting tiresome. She was a sweet girl, but where the hell was Catie? This was her damn party, after all. Chad's black lab, Marnie, panted at his feet. He gave her a quick pet. "Thatsa girl. You thirsty? I'll see about gettin' you some water."

"Hey, Chad." The husky drawl came from his brother Dallas.

"Dallas, hey."

"Who you got here?"

"This is Amber Cross. Amber, my brother Dallas."

"Nice to meet you," Amber said.

"You too." Dallas shook Amber's hand and patted Marnie's soft head. "Has this brother of mine told you what he's doing next weekend?"

"What am I doing next weekend?" Chad said.

"Judging the rodeo queen competition. How quickly you forget."

"Damn." Chad thumped himself on the forehead. "I actually did forget. Is there something I need to do?"

"Just get ready to eye the beauty of Bakersville, little brother."

"Rodeo queen?" Amber's light brown eyes lit up. "What's that about, Chad?"

"Bakersville's answer to a beauty queen, honey. Nothin' you'd be interested in."

"Why not?"

"That's my cue to leave, I think." Dallas walked away, chuckling.

"Damn, brother," Chad said under his breath. Now he'd started something.

"I just might enter this contest," Amber said.

"Can't. You're too old."

"What do you mean I'm too old? You don't even know how old I am."

"You have to be between eighteen and twenty-two. And single."

"Well, of course you know I'm single," Amber said. "What makes you think I'm too old?"

Jesus. He'd walked right into that one. "Now, honey, you're beautiful, but you can't possibly be—"

Amber's face reddened, and she reached into the small pocketbook hanging at her hip. She pulled out her wallet and then her driver's license and shoved it in Chad's face. "I'm twenty-one, you dumb cowboy. Twenty-two next month. So I qualify. And I'm entering."

"Christ," Chad muttered. Twenty-one? He'd had no idea. Twenty-one. Catie's age.

Damn.

Somehow, though, with Amber, the age didn't pack quite as much of a wallop as it did with Catie. Maybe because he remembered what Catie looked like at five. He shook his head.

Damn it all to hell.

"Clearly, I look like an old bat to you," Amber yammered in his ear.

"No, that's not it at all," Chad said. "I just assumed... Aw hell, there's no getting out of this one, is there?"

"Afraid not, Chad," she said.

"Let me get you a drink, then," he said. "I've found women find my foot in my mouth much more charming when they've had a drink."

Amber's lips curved upward. *Yep, the McCray charm worked every time.* "All right, I guess."

"Forgive me, then?"

"Sure, I suppose."

"Let me get you that drink. What'll you—" His mouth

dropped open.

In a clingy red sundress leaving nothing to the imagination stood Catie Bay. Nothing to the imagination except the hue of those pert nipples protruding through the silky fabric. Pink? Or a deeper crimson? Maybe a dusky brown? And the color of the curls between her legs. Were they dark mahogany, like on her head? Or black as onyx?

His jeans tightened around his groin. Damn, her legs went on forever. Those luscious thighs disappeared under that clingy red skirt, and all Chad could think about was the sweet, moist spot at their apex. Would that taste like lime and raspberries too?

"A cosmo," came a voice from far away. "Or white wine, if they don't have mixed drinks."

Who was that?

Amber. Right. He'd offered to get her a drink. A bar had been set up on the deck...where Catie was headed.

"Right. I'll get it." Not looking at Amber, he headed toward the bar. And Catie.

"Hey, little bit."

"Hey yourself," Catie said, leaning down to pet Marnie, "and I thought you promised not to call me that anymore."

Chad chuckled. "Old habits die hard, Catie."

"Caitlyn."

"Right. Caitlyn. Drinking 'ritas again?"

Catie smiled. Had she always had those cute little dimples?

"I'm sticking to iced tea tonight. For a while, anyway."

The bartender handed her a tall glass of tea. "There you are, gorgeous."

The muscles in Chad's jaw tensed. Who the hell was he,

anyway, calling her that?

"See you later, Chad." She walked away, her hips swaying gently beneath her silky sheath.

"What can I get you?" the bartender asked.

"You can keep your hands off her, first of all," Chad said, between clenched teeth.

"Sorry. She your girlfriend?"

"No."

"Your sister?"

"Hell, no."

"Then what's the problem?"

"She's...aw, hell, I don't have to explain myself to you. Give me a...what the hell is that froufrou pink martini called again?"

"A cosmo?"

"Yeah, that's the one. A cosmo. And a Fat Tire. Damn, make that two."

He chugged the first one and took the remaining beer and the cosmo back to Amber.

And there was Catie again, chatting away with Amber.

Damn it all to fucking hell.

★ ★ ★

He was walking toward them, Marnie at his heels. It had taken every ounce of strength Catie possessed to act so nonchalantly at the bar. She was secretly thrilled when the hunky bartender called her gorgeous and hoped Chad had noticed. Then Amber had called her over, and it would have been rude to ignore her. She really was a nice girl, even though her platinum blond hooks were sunk in the cowboy Catie wanted more than her next breath of air.

"Thank you, Chad," Amber said, when Chad handed her the cosmo. "Did you know Caitlyn's entering the rodeo queen contest too?"

"Christ," Chad said. "What is it with you two? That contest is stupid."

"Then why'd you agree to judge it?" Catie asked.

"I got forced into it?"

"By whom?" Amber asked.

"By my brothers. By the mayor of Bakersville. By the whole damn universe. Sheesh."

"Calm down, goodness," Amber said. "According to Caitlyn, it's quite an honor to judge the thing. And an honor to win, as well."

"Catie, what the hell are you filling her full of?" Chad took a swig of his beer.

"Nothing, Chad. I've lived here almost my whole life, and you know what a huge thing our rodeo is. It's the pride of Bakersville, and it's every little girl's dream to represent the town at the rodeo."

"I'd bet it was never your dream," he said. "Your dream was to ride like the wind atop your mare. Ladybird, right?"

"Well, I have to admit, I never considered it before. But I've been gone for a while, Chad. I think it would be an honor to represent my town as rodeo queen. I think it would mean a lot to Amber, too, being new here."

"Yes, it certainly would," Amber said. "Do you know who else is entered?"

"I have no idea," Catie said. "I just got back in town. Chad probably knows, don't you?"

"I haven't the foggiest."

"But you're a judge."

"So? Doesn't mean I give two damns, sugar."

Sugar. He'd called her sugar again. Oh, the sweet sound of it. And from Amber's pursed lips, clearly she'd noticed, too. Course it probably didn't sound nearly so sweet to her. Catie couldn't help but smile.

"Well, I expect you'll be a terrible judge then," she said. "Thank goodness Zach and Dallas will take this duty more seriously."

Chad let out a belly laugh. "You're kidding right, Catie?"

"Caitlyn."

"Christ. *Caitlyn.* Do you really think Zach and Dallas care any more about this thing than I do?"

"This is a tradition in Bakersville. It's part of our history. It's a...a..." Catie grasped for words. "It's as true to Bakersville as the Miss America pageant is to Atlantic City. Just ask Annie. That's where she's from!"

"I can't imagine Dr. Annie having anything to do with pageants of any kind, Catie."

She scoffed, and he rolled his eyes.

"*Caitlyn.* And as far as this one, I got roped into judging, and I'll do it, but neither of you better expect any preferential treatment from me. I intend to be fully fair and impartial." He shook his head. "Of all the silly nonsense. Especially you, Catie. I'd've thought you'd have more sense."

Anger seethed in Catie's gut. It was as much an insult to Amber as it was to her, but if he thought she'd have more sense, why did he insist on thinking of her as a child? How dare he belittle her? "You've already told me I'm just a kid. I believe those were your words last evening, if I recall correctly. So it makes perfect sense that I'd want to take part in this silly tradition. Amber, I'll leave this jerk to you."

Catie stormed off, across the yard, her sandals tapping on the patio, through the kitchen where the caterers were readying the buffet, up the stairs, and to her pink and horsy room. She flopped onto her bed and let the anger give way to sadness. She hugged her stuffed horse as tears fell.

Tears for missing four years of her life in Bakersville. Tears for Laurie McCray, her second mother, whose funeral she hadn't attended. Tears of jealousy for Annie, who had her handsome McCray boy and his children. Tears for Amber, whom she liked, and who might have been a friend under different circumstances. And mostly tears for her unrequited love. Even four years in Europe hadn't erased him from her heart.

She sobbed and sniffed into her pillow as she realized the bitter truth.

Nothing would ever erase Chad McCray from her heart.

CHAPTER FIVE

Catie wasn't sure how much time had passed. Surely the caterers would have dinner ready by now. Still, she lay on her bed. The sobs had stopped, replaced by sniffles. She grabbed tissue after tissue from her nightstand until her bed was a sea of used snot rags.

She let out a heavy sigh. Her door creaked open.

"Sugar?"

Oh God. Not Chad. He couldn't see her like this. In this infantile bedroom that belonged to a horse-loving freckle-faced teenager.

"Your ma's looking for you. I told her I'd find you. It's almost time for the buffet."

His voice was husky and sexy. Same as always. Same as freaking always.

"Go away, Chad. Please."

"Have you been crying? Damn, what's wrong?"

He walked in and sat down on her bed. She turned toward the wall, inching away from him.

"I'm sure sorry, sugar. I didn't mean to upset you. If you really want to be rodeo queen, you'll be the prettiest one ever. I swear it."

"Please go away."

"Not until you get your pretty self up and come down and join your party."

She shuddered when the warmth of his hand caressed her

back.

He rubbed her slowly, comfortingly. "Come on."

She turned toward him. She couldn't hide forever. He'd never love her, so what did it matter if she looked a fright? "Give me a minute, okay? Where's Marnie?"

"I'll give you all the time you need. Marnie's down there playing with her cousins." He laughed. "Seanie and the twins, that is." He got up, walked to her dressing table, and retrieved her brush. He sat down, pulled a red bandana out of his pocket, wiped her tears, and held it over her nose. "Blow."

She giggled. Chad McCray, the love of her short life, was holding a hanky for her to blow her nose into. What else was there to do but laugh? She blew as daintily as she could, which wasn't very. She'd always been a honker.

"There, that's better." He stuffed the bandana back in his pocket. "Sit up now."

She obeyed, and surprise gushed through her as he began to brush her long hair.

"I remember when this pretty hair was always in two pigtails, and that cute little nose of yours was covered in freckles." Chad's touch was so gentle as he brushed. Even with the snarls, he didn't pull once. "Whatever happened to that little girl I once knew?"

Catie gulped. "She grew up."

Chad put the brush down on the nightstand and cupped both Catie's cheeks in his hands. "She sure did, sugar. You're about the most beautiful woman I've ever laid eyes on."

Her heart thundered, and butterflies flew around in her tummy. Had he just called her beautiful? Her eyes swollen from crying, her nose still congested? Beautiful? Her lips shook as she spoke. "Ch-Chad?"

He brushed one calloused thumb over her bottom lip. "These are the softest, sweetest lips I've ever kissed, too." He smiled a crooked smile.

Had Catie not known better, she'd have thought it was a shy smile.

"Have you let a lot of men kiss these lips?"

"N-Not too many," Catie stammered.

"I'm right glad to hear that, sugar," Chad said, and replaced his thumb with his lips. He brushed over her lips gently, slowly nibbling, taking only the smallest taste. She closed her eyes and savored the masculine feel of him. His tongue peeked out and traced her lips, and a soft sigh escaped her throat.

"Mmm, sugar," he said against her mouth. "You still taste like raspberries. Raspberries and sweet tea."

"Th-That's what I've been drinking. Raspberry tea."

He chuckled. "You tasted like raspberries last night, and you were drinking 'ritas. It's just the sweet flavor of you, Caitlyn."

She couldn't help smiling. It sounded all wrong. "Catie."

"Catie it is, then." He crushed his mouth onto hers.

The kiss was open-mouthed, wet, and hungry, and she responded with her whole body and heart. She reached for Chad's head and tunneled her fingers through his thick hair. Silk, just as she'd always imagined. She let the strands sift through her fingers and then she grabbed the back of his head and pulled him closer. Their mouths already meshed together, they kissed frantically, their tongues tangling. A low rumble escaped Chad's throat.

His hand crept from her shoulder to her breast, and he stroked it through the thin fabric of her dress. Her nipple puckered, and she leaned into him, wanting to feel his hard chest against hers.

When he ripped his mouth from hers, she whimpered.

"Damn," he said. "What the hell am I doing?"

"I don't know," Catie said, "but please don't stop."

"Catie, this is all wrong."

"No. No, Chad, it's not wrong. It's right. It's so very, very right. It's all I've ever wanted."

Chad kissed her cheek. A sweet, loving kiss. "You have a schoolgirl crush on me, Catie. That's all. And right now, what I'm feeling for you goes way beyond what a schoolboy feels. I'm a man, with man feelings and man desires."

"Chad, please." She held his head in his hands and looked into his burning gaze. "I'm not a schoolgirl. I'm a woman."

"And I'm a man, sugar, and right now this man has got some very strong desires to take you to bed and ravish that gorgeous body of yours."

"Then do it."

"God, sugar." He groaned, covered her hands with his, and removed them from his face. "I can't do it. As much as I want you, I just can't."

"Why not?"

"'Cause then I'd have to marry you, and I don't want to marry anybody."

Catie's heart fell. There. He'd said it. He didn't want to marry her. Didn't want to marry anyone, for that matter. But he wanted her. She inhaled, bracing herself for a fight she intended to win. It wasn't forever, but it was a start.

"Why? Why would you have to marry me, Chad? That's the silliest thing I've ever heard."

"Because"—he stroked her cheek—"you're better than a one-shot roll in the hay, sugar. I won't do that to you."

"Better? Better than what? What makes me better than any other woman, Chad? Better than Amber? Because I'm pretty sure you've rolled in that hay with her."

"Amber? Heck no, sugar. We're just friends."

"So you never considered—"

"Hell, yeah, I considered it, and then I decided against it. I...aw hell, Catie. Yeah, I was ready to. I was ready to screw the daylights out of her last night. Until you came along."

"Me."

"Yeah, you. Once I set eyes on you, Amber had no appeal. You turned those pretty brown eyes on me, and I melted. But damn it, I won't—"

Catie cut him off with a kiss. A kiss so deep and powerful, she felt as though their souls had fused. She poured seventeen years of love for Chad McCray into that kiss. Seventeen years of longing and desire, hoping against hope that he'd return it, if only for a second or two.

He did.

He kissed her with an urgency she'd never felt. He bit her lower lip, sucked it between his teeth. He tangled her tongue with his, explored every crevice of her mouth. All this time he moaned, he groaned, his husky voice rumbled as he nipped at her, tasted her, drank her in, made passionate love to her mouth.

Catie had never imagined such a kiss. A kiss that not only gave, but took. A kiss that heated her body and caused havoc between her legs. A kiss nearly as intimate as the sexual act itself.

After a few breathless moments, the passion slowed, and Chad moved his lips to her cheek, raining tiny kisses across her face, her neck. Catie shuddered as sparks erupted everywhere his lips touched.

"Chad, Chad," she said. "This feels so good. So nice."

"You ain't felt nothin' yet, sugar." Chad traced the shell of her ear with his hot tongue. "Damn, you're something, Catie. It's been a long time since I've wanted a woman this much."

"Take me, Chad. Please."

"Aw, sugar. I can't." He fingered the wisp of her spaghetti strap and eased it down over her shoulder. He kissed her sensitive skin, leaving tingles everywhere. His calloused hands reached for the other strap, and soon the bodice of her sheath dropped to her waist, exposing her breasts.

Chad sucked in a breath. "Coppery-brown, like the bricks on the walkway to my place."

"What?"

"Your nipples, sugar. They're beautiful. And they're all puckered up and hard for me." He moved her hands from her shoulders, but stopped before settling them on her breasts. "If I taste those pretty nipples, there's no going back. I won't be able to stop. I'll need to make love to you. All the way, baby. Are you sure you want that?"

"God, yes, Chad. It's all I've ever wanted."

"You know I can't marry you."

"Geez, I'm not asking for a marriage proposal."

"You deserve one, Catie, but it won't come from me. I'm sorry."

"It's okay. For God's sake, Chad, just get on with it."

"Tell me you've done this before, sugar. You've slept with a man."

"Uh...yeah, sure I have."

"Okay. Are you sure you want this?"

"Damn it, how many times do I have to say it?"

He chuckled. "One more ought to do it."

"Okay then." She smiled at him and tried her darnedest to look as though the whole marriage thing meant nothing to her. Hoping he couldn't read all the lies in her eyes. "I want this. I want you." She tried not to choke on the words. "I understand you won't marry me."

"Thank God. As long as we're on the same page." He lowered his mouth to her nipple and kissed it.

A jolt shot through Catie like a streak of lightning. She already knew the warm softness of those lips on hers, but on the sensitive turgid flesh of her nipple, they sparked heat to every cell of her body.

"Mmm," Chad said against her flesh, "these taste even better than they look." He closed his teeth around her nipple and tugged.

She gasped. Pleasure flowed through her like warm honey and settled between her legs. She closed her eyes and leaned her head backward, the whisper of her long tresses a tickle against her bare skin.

"Catie?"

Chad's head popped up. "Shit!" He quickly pulled Catie's dress over her breasts and settled her straps back over her shoulders. "Someone's coming."

"Catie?" Her mother's voice cut through her closed door.

"Yeah, Mama?"

"Aren't you coming down, sweetie? It's dinner time."

"Yeah, sure, Mama." She cleared her throat. "I'll be right there. Give me two minutes, okay?"

"Are you okay? You sound funny." The doorknob turned slightly.

"Oh, I'm fine. Just still a little jet-lagged, is all. I won't be a minute."

"All right. Hurry up, though. We want to get started."

With the click of her mother's footsteps fading, Catie breathed a sigh of relief.

"That was close."

"A little too close," Chad agreed, "but probably for the best."

"How do you mean?"

"Sugar, we were about to do something we both would have regretted."

Catie's heart sank. He would regret it? "Oh."

"Now don't you give me that long face." He caressed her cheek with his thumb. "This worked out for the best. I hope you can forgive me."

"There's nothing to forgive, Chad. I wanted it as much as you did." Probably more, but she didn't say it.

"Well, no harm done." He stood and helped her to her feet. "Now you look pretty as a picture. Let's go get some of those eats, okay?"

She nodded, choking back the tears that threatened. Sure, she'd go eat. It would all taste like sawdust, but what the heck?

"You go on down," Chad was saying, "and I'll follow in ten minutes or so."

She nodded again, looked in her mirror. Her eyes were still puffy but there wasn't anything she could do about it. She brushed her hair, applied some lipstick and then some soothing eye gel that would hopefully ease the puffiness. She glanced at Chad one more time, said nothing, opened her bedroom door, and headed down to the party.

★ ★ ★

Chad flopped back on Catie's pink comforter. His erection throbbed beneath his belt buckle. Whew. Saved by the bell.

But damn, he hadn't wanted to be saved. He'd wanted nothing more than to sink himself into her softness.

He wasn't sure he'd ever wanted a woman as much as he longed for Catie Bay. He rubbed his palm over his denim-clad erection and groaned. What the hell had he been thinking?

He'd been thinking she was the prettiest thing he'd seen this side of heaven. That's what he'd been thinking. With the perkiest breasts and sweetest nipples he'd ever tasted. What was it about her? His pulse still stampeded. He loved women, and he loved sex, but his pulse didn't usually race. His skin didn't usually tingle. What the hell was going on?

Damn, if she walked back in this room in the next minute, he'd be all over her again.

He got up quickly, raked his fingers through his mass of hair, and wondered what to do about the throbbing in his pants. A cold shower was out of the question. Maria could walk in and find him, or worse yet, Harper or Wayne.

He shook his head. He'd have to deal with the discomfort and will it down himself.

He went down to join the others and tried not to stare at Catie, who had taken a seat at a table with her parents, Harper, and Dallas and Annie and their two daughters.

Of course, it'd be perfectly acceptable to join them. Dallas was his brother, after all.

"Uncle Chad!"

His four-year-old nephew, Sean, ran toward him. Sean had a shock of strawberry blond hair that matched his mother's and two light blue eyes. He was a beautiful kid, and was the one who'd first made Chad an uncle. Chad had a special place in his heart for Sean.

"Hey, little critter, where's your ma and pa?"

"They're gettin' food. But I saw you and wanted to hang out with you."

"Aw." Chad's heart melted.

"When are we goin' fishin' again?" The little boy asked.

Chad scooped up his nephew and started for the buffet. "Anytime, critter, anytime. We'll catch us some good Rocky Mountain trout, won't we? For now, though, let's get some chow."

"Okay," he said, his little hands grasping Chad's shoulders.

Chad filled a plate for himself and for Sean and then went to join Zach and Dusty, Sean's parents, at a table that was, thankfully, far from Catie's.

He gazed at his pretty sister-in-law and marveled at how much Sean looked like her. Except for those blue eyes. They were from his pa, but only one of them. Chad's brother Zach had one brown eye and one blue. Didn't bother Dusty, though. She was crazy in love with him, and the feeling was mutual. It showed all over both their faces.

For a minute Chad wondered what it would feel like to have a woman crazy in love with him. Would she look at him with stars in her eyes the way Dusty looked at Zach, even after nearly five years together?

Even more surreal, how would it feel to him to be crazy in love with a woman? Would he stare at his woman dreamily, the way Zach stared at Dusty? The way Dallas stared at Annie? His brothers were goners, for sure.

Course neither of them had been the womanizer Chad

was. Neither dated in high school, while Chad had been all over the cheerleaders and 4-H girls. Dallas had married an eastern girl, only to divorce her years later. He met and married Annie soon after his divorce was final. Zach had been briefly engaged to Catie's older sister, Angie, but that hadn't worked out. Neither had known love until they'd met their current wives.

And neither ceased to extol the virtues of married life with the right woman.

Chad was damn sick of hearing it.

"Uncle Chad's takin' me fishin'," Sean said, interrupting Chad's thoughts. The little boy munched on a corncob.

"Don't talk with your mouth open, sweetie," Dusty said. "That's nice of you, Chad. He sure had fun the last time."

"I did, too," Chad said truthfully. "I love hanging out with the critter."

Yep, he sure was a dead ringer for his pretty ma. Chad stole a glance across the yard at Catie's table, where Dallas and Annie sat with their twin girls. Those pretty little things looked just like their daddy.

For just a flash, an image burned into Chad's mind. He held a little boy with mahogany hair and brown eyes. A little boy who looked at him the way Sean was looking at Zach right now. With blind adoration.

Hell, what was he thinking? He didn't want a kid. And he sure as hell didn't want a wife.

Try as he might, though, the image niggled at the back of his mind the rest of the dinner and beyond.

His pulse raced and his skin tingled as the face on his wife became clear in his imaginary family portrait.

This wasn't normal.

He needed to stay far away from Catie Bay.

CHAPTER SIX

The party had been fun, Catie had to admit, even though her heart had fallen just a little bit more when she'd spied Chad leaving with Amber. But her spirits were renewed a bit when she saw the moon rise full in the sky overhead.

Four long years had passed since she'd taken Ladybird on a moonlight ride. She headed into the house to change into riding clothes, and then to the barn where she saddled the mare. They took off together, riding as one through the warm summer night.

Her Stetson fell off her head and dangled around her neck by the strings as she and Ladybird galloped through the breeze. Her hair whipped about her face. It would be a mass of snarls when she returned, but she didn't care.

She had missed this. How had she stayed away so long?

As she neared the border of the McCray land, another rider slipped into her view. Probably a hired hand checking things out for the night.

Her heart leaped as she rode closer. A black lab ran beside the rider. *Marnie.* And she knew those shoulders. That broad back. They belonged to the youngest, tallest, and best looking of the McCrays. Her tummy did a little tumble. He was out on a night ride rather than in Amber's bed, finishing what he'd started with Catie.

Chad.

He turned around when she and Ladybird trotted toward

him. His gorgeous black gelding kicked at the earth.

"Looks like we had the same idea," Catie said.

"Hey, sugar. I guess so."

"Want to ride together?"

He smiled, and his golden skin glowed in the luminescence of the full moon. "Sure. I 'spose so. Wouldn't mind the company."

"New horse?" Catie didn't recognize him.

"Yeah, this is Eclipse. I call him that 'cause he's black as night."

"He's beautiful."

"That he is. So is your lady."

"Yeah." Catie smiled. What a beautiful night. "Let's ride."

They galloped together across the vastness of the Colorado plains. Stars sparkled across the clear sky, and the full moon illuminated the majestic Rockies in translucent indigo against the horizon.

Oh, she had missed this.

After an hour of hard riding, they stopped to let their horses rest.

"I should see you home, Catie," Chad said. "It's nearing two."

"I know," she said softly, "but it's such a beautiful night. I'm not sure I want to go in. I don't want to lose the magic of it."

"Silly," he chuckled. "Colorado has a night like this once or twice a month. We live in the most beautiful land in the world."

"Yeah, I know."

"If it's so beautiful, why'd you stay away so long?"

"Mmm. Don't know."

"I think you do. You said you'd tell me sometime."

"Maybe I will. Maybe I won't."

"How about now?"

"How about we ride back?" she said, climbing atop Ladybird.

"All right, I can take a hint. It's late, and I'm going to see you safely home, sugar."

"Not necessary." Though she was secretly ecstatic to spend a little more time with him. "I know this land like the back of my hand."

"As do I, and I'm coming with you."

"If you insist."

"I do." He climbed on Eclipse and they rode toward the Bay land, keeping the horses to a canter, and not saying much.

Catie reveled in being with him. The man she loved.

They reached the Bay barn and Chad helped her curry down Ladybird and get her bedded.

"Thanks for riding with me," she said. "I sure had fun."

"Me too, sugar."

He grinned, and her heart stopped. God, he was so handsome. Always had been, but now...he damn near robbed her of breath.

She expected him to get on Eclipse and high tail it out of there faster than a jackrabbit, but instead he took her into his arms and gave her a brotherly hug. The warmth of his body, flushed from the excitement of the ride, made her tingle all over with prickly needles.

And then the hug was no longer brotherly. His lips pressed to her neck in moist kisses. "Why can't I keep my hands to myself around you, sugar?"

"Mmm," she said. "I don't know, but I'm glad you can't."

"All I want to do," he rasped, sliding his mouth over her

cheeks, her eyelids, her forehead, "is finish what we started in your room today. But it would be a powerful mistake."

"Mmm. Why is that again?"

"Because you deserve more than a roll in the hay."

Catie erupted in giggles.

"What's so funny, sugar?"

"A roll in the hay. Chad, we're in a barn."

He chuckled. "We sure are. And I sure as hell am not going to love your sweet body for the first time in a stinky old barn."

"Where then?" The bold statement surprised her, even after it had escaped her lips.

Chad paused and stared at her. She grabbed a broom and swept Ladybird's stall to give her hands something to do.

Then he spoke. "Back to my place."

"But my parents... They'll wonder where I am."

"You're fond of telling me what a grown-up girl you are, sugar. They didn't know where the heck you were or what you were doing the last four years. Come on, you can ride with me on Eclipse."

"Chad—"

"Come on now, Catie. I can't wait another minute to have you."

He helped her mount Eclipse, climbed up behind her, and they rode into the still night.

He kept the horse to a trot, and Catie let her head fall back against Chad's hard chest. His powerful muscular thighs hugged hers. Every part of her was hyper-aware, hyper-conscious of the man behind her, the man in control of the beautiful animal atop which she sat.

It will happen. Tonight.

Tonight she would make love with Chad McCray.

★ ★ ★

Back at Chad's house, Catie stared in awe. She'd been to the main house, which dwarfed her ranch house. But this one... Was it bigger? Or had she spent too many years in quaint Paris townhouses?

Within seconds, Chad had scooped her into his arms and carried her to what she presumed was his bedroom. He deposited her on his bed, took off his boots and socks, throwing them to the other side of the room, and unsnapped his western shirt. She gulped as he exposed his chest. Pure golden muscle, accented with dark brown hair smattered over his pecs. The hair grew lighter until it disappeared in a line under his belt buckle. She gulped again. A bulge under his belt buckle beckoned her.

A really *big* bulge.

"Sugar, those eyes are about as big as flying saucers. You all right?"

"Oh, yeah. Sure. I'm just—"

"Stop me now, if you're going to. Because once these pants come off, there'll be no going back."

"I don't want to stop."

"Thank God." He yanked open the snaps on her shirt, unhooked her bra, and let her breasts fall against her chest. He sucked in his breath. "I'm going to kiss every inch of your gorgeous body tonight, sugar. I'm going to taste every ounce of honey you have to offer."

Catie shuddered. His sexy words embarrassed her, yet inflamed her. She wanted to hear more. She wanted to feel more. His lips everywhere. On her mouth, her nipples, between her legs.

Oh God...

Chad pulled her boots off one by one, and then her socks. He reached forward and unbuckled her belt, unzipped her jeans, and pulled them off, along with her already moist panties, until they joined her blouse and bra in a heap on the floor.

"I've never seen anyone more beautiful," he said. "It's a crime to cover your body, sugar." He cupped her breasts. "These are works of art. Big, but not too big. Perfect rusty nipples."

He thumbed them, and a jolt shot between Catie's legs.

"Just like sweet berries under my tongue." He lowered his head and sucked, licking and tugging.

Catie shook with want and anticipation. "Chad. Make love to me. Please."

"I plan to. But like I said, not until I taste every inch of you."

And he did. Starting with her mouth. He swirled his tongue with hers, mating, dancing, kissing her with a reckless abandon Catie had never known. He rained kisses on her cheeks, her ears, dipped his tongue into her ear and Catie tingled all over. He sucked on her neck, her breasts, and then bit her nipples until she cried out in pain that morphed into pleasure. His talented mouth traveled down her chest and belly, and stopped at her nest of curls as he inhaled.

"Black, like mine," he said, smiling up at her, their eyes meeting.

"Wh-What?"

"I wondered what color your hair was down here.

Whether it was the same color as your head, or darker."

"Oh." She had no idea men thought about things like that. She'd never once wondered what color his pubic hair was. But now she itched to find out. Course he'd already said it was black, like hers.

"Open your legs for me, sugar. Let me see that pretty flesh."

She obeyed, embarrassed, yet wanting to share her whole self with him.

"Ah, beautiful," he said. "You glisten, sugar. Glisten with sweet honey."

He ran one finger over her slick folds, and she cried out, sinking her head farther into his pillow.

"So wet, sugar. So wet for me."

"Chad, please."

"What, baby?"

"I want you. Inside me. Please come inside me."

"Oh, I will, sure as the day is long. But first..." His tongue darted out and slithered over her wetness.

Catie's body quivered. Had anything ever felt quite so amazing? She couldn't tell Chad, but no man had kissed her there before. In fact, she wasn't sure why he wanted to do it, but he certainly seemed to be enjoying himself. God knew it felt like heaven from her end.

He sucked and licked, driving her into a frenzy, the erotic sounds he made landing at the back of her neck and sending chills through her heated body. She rose higher, and higher still, until a thousand sparks erupted on her skin and soared inward, igniting every cell of her body in a delicious euphoric blaze. She reveled, crying out Chad's name, writhing on the bed in time with his worship of her. When she finally floated downward, Chad was working two fingers in and out of her, and the soothing caress, to the most intimate part of her, churned her desire once more.

Delicious. Heady. Amazing.

This was an orgasm. It had to be. How wonderful that her handsome cowboy, the man she had loved from afar for so long, would be the one to give it to her.

"Good, sugar?"

He smiled, and for a moment she imagined the sun itself shone through his face.

"More than good."

"I was right, you know."

"Mmm. Right about what?"

"You taste like raspberries down here, too." He licked his lips.

Catie warmed, and rosiness crept up her belly to her breasts.

"Don't be embarrassed, sugar." He smiled again, his chin slick with her juices.

She shuddered.

"I enjoyed every single minute of it. In fact, I wouldn't mind diving back in for—"

"No, Chad."

"No?"

"I mean, I loved it. I truly did. But I need you inside me. I've wanted you there for so long."

He stood up, and Catie focused on his hands as they unbuckled his belt and unzipped his jeans.

For a split second, "boxers or briefs" flew through her mind, and she couldn't help giggling.

"Laughing, sugar?" He smiled. "You'll give me a complex."

His jeans hit the floor, and she had an answer. Boxer briefs. Forest-green cotton boxer briefs that molded to the most shapely rear end and most muscular thighs she'd ever seen.

But those male model goodies paled in comparison to the bulge. A small spot of wetness appeared where the head of his cock peeked out.

She sucked in her breath and widened her eyes as he slowly peeled the underwear from his ripped body.

His erection sprang from a thick bush of black hair. God Almighty, he was huge. Catie wasn't experienced by a long shot, but she'd seen a few in her day. This one was monstrous. In a good way. He reached into his nightstand drawer, pulled out a condom, and quickly sheathed his cock.

"I take it I haven't disappointed you."

"You could never disappoint me," she said, and meant it.

He lowered himself next to her on the bed and teased her nipples with his lips. "I hope you won't regret this, sugar, because no matter what happens, I can tell you for damn sure that I won't. You are a treasure. A true treasure."

He kissed her mouth then. A firm, possessive kiss, and she wrapped her arms around his neck and pulled him on top of her.

She gasped when he plunged into her. It hurt. More than she'd expected. But then he was unusually large.

"Catie?"

"Yeah. I'm fine."

"But you said—"

"You wouldn't have made love to me otherwise." She shut her eyes, wincing at what felt like her flesh tearing. "I'm fine. Really. Just...go ahead."

"Aw damn." He surged forward until he was embedded deep inside her, and then he stilled. "I need to give you a minute to adjust, okay?"

She nodded. "Okay."

"You let me know when I can move."

"I'm fine, Chad. You can move. I... I want this. I wanted it to be you."

"I can't take your virginity, Catie."

"You already have."

"Damn. Goddamn it."

She opened her eyes. Chad's teeth were clenched, his facial muscles taut. Sweat trickled from his brow. Was he in as much pain as she was?

"I want this, Chad."

"Well, there's nothing we can do about it now."

"I know. I'm fine. I'm ready. The pain is gone. I just feel... full."

That seemed to relax him, and he chuckled. "You are full, baby, and God but you feel good."

Catie breathed deeply and delighted in his hard body covering hers, his chest hair tickling her tender nipples. "Love me. Please, Chad. I want this to be good for you."

"Oh, it will be." He pulled out and thrust back into her. "I'll make it good for you, too."

"It's already good for me. Just because it's you."

He thrust again, and the friction of him moving in her became less of a burn and more of a sweet sting. A sting that sent tiny ripples of bliss coursing through her.

"Damn, sugar, you're so tight."

He surged again, and again, and once more still, until Catie closed her eyes and felt the tingles creeping along her skin again. "Chad," she cried. "Chad, that's it. Chad!"

Swirling rainbows enveloped her as Chad continued to plunge into her. She heard herself screaming, whispering, and screaming again. His mouth covered hers and he kissed her, his tongue thrusting in tandem with his cock. Her body flew into spasms, and as one orgasm ended another began, and then again, and again.

Finally, as the last one subsided, Chad grunted and pushed deep into her, his body tensing atop hers. "Catie. Sweet Catie."

He rolled over onto his side and pushed a stray hair out of her eyes. "You should have told me."

"You already thought I was a little kid."

"Being a virgin's nothing to be ashamed of, sugar. It's sweet, actually. None of those randy Frenchmen tried anything with you?"

"Oh, they tried."

He smiled and then left the bed. He pulled off his condom and threw it toward the wastebasket next to his night table. "I'll be right back."

He returned with a warm cloth, and with exquisite care, he cleaned her.

"Did I bleed?"

"Only a little. Nothing to worry about."

The soft, warm cloth soothed her sore tissues.

"Gosh, you sure are pretty down here, Catie. All pink and swollen. All I can think about is making love to you again."

She smiled. "Go ahead."

"You need to heal, sugar. It'll be a few days until we can do this again. It might not be such a good idea, anyway."

"Why on earth not? I told you already you don't have to

marry me."

"Yeah, well..." Chad stood up, threw the rag in his hamper by the foot of the bed, and lay back down next to her. "You may change your mind about that."

"Why would I?"

"Because a girl like you—" He chuckled at her pout. "A classy woman like you, I mean, deserves better than one night of passion."

"Okay, I'll take two nights of passion."

"Sugar—"

"I'll take as many nights of passion as you're willing to give me. I've never asked you for more."

"No, you haven't."

"I won't even ask for special treatment in the rodeo queen competition." She winked.

"Heck. You still on that kick?"

"Yeah."

"I don't know, sugar. It might be too late to enter."

"Dallas said he'd get me in." She yawned. "And I'm gonna win, too."

He chuckled and ran his fingers over her cheek. "You're tired as a mule in a horse race, sugar. Probably still jet-lagging. Go to sleep, okay? I'll take you home in the morning."

Catie nodded, and snuggled up to Chad's hard body.

A few hours later, she awoke to Chad's arm slung across her waist.

Home. She had to get home. Before dawn would be the best, though she was twenty-one, and she sure shouldn't have to answer to her parents about where she'd been.

She could borrow one of Chad's horses and be home before sunup.

As delicately as she could, she eased Chad's arm away from her.

He tightened his hold on her in response.

"Mmm. Catie." His voice was husky and sleep filled. His eyes didn't open.

"Chad?"

No response.

Yeah, he was asleep.

She attempted to nudge his arm away again.

"Mmm. Stay with me," he murmured. "I've waited so long for you." He let out a soft snore.

He was asleep. Dreaming, no doubt. Catie's pulse raced anyway, and warm joy surged through her.

I've waited so long for you.

Was he thinking of her? Dreaming of her?

She turned her head and kissed the hard muscles of his upper arm that held her bound.

She'd gladly stay.

Forever, if he'd have her.

CHAPTER SEVEN

Catie awoke, and for a moment, didn't know where she was. The soreness between her legs jogged her memory. Chad had taken her virginity last night.

Chad.

She jerked up and looked around the room. He was gone. Well, he couldn't have gone far. Catie stretched and relished the warmth from the sun's summer rays entering the bay window in Chad's bedroom. She looked around. Hadn't bothered to last night.

This was Chad's room all right. Shades of hunter green and mahogany veiled his walnut furniture. The beautiful bedstead was ornately carved. Not something she thought Chad would choose. It looked almost antique. She made a mental note to ask him about it. She got up and walked around, still stark naked. On his dresser rested several trophies from rodeo events. She'd known Chad for years, though, and this couldn't be the extent of his trophies. No doubt he had a whole room full of them somewhere in this giant house.

His closet was open, and she peeked in. The size of a small office, it was filled with mostly jeans and western shirts. She chuckled aloud at the thirty-two pairs of cowboy boots she counted. Who said only women had a thing for shoes? Truth to tell, boots and shoes combined, Catie's collection didn't equal near thirty-two. She never was a clotheshorse like her sister, Angie. Give her a pair of worn in boots and jeans, a comfy cotton shirt, and she was set.

She padded into Chad's private bathroom, took care of necessities, and looked in the mirror.

What a sight.

Hair snarled from the night ride, raccoon eyes from the mascara she'd donned for the party.

Yuck. She rubbed at her eyes. No more mascara. Ever. Even for that damn rodeo queen contest. There was a reason she never wore the stuff. She'd just forgotten for a few brainless moments.

And her cheeks and neck and breasts, all ruddy from Chad's whisker burn. Her nipples were dark and tender. She cupped her breasts and held them up. They looked, and felt, well loved.

She let out a quick breath. She needed a shower. A long, slow, hot shower to soothe her muscles and the tender spot between her legs. She'd ridden a little while she'd been abroad, but not nearly enough to stay in shape. Two rides on Ladybird yesterday had turned her thighs into throbbing jelly. Her shoulders ached too, and her neck. She shook her head. She should have known better, but she'd missed this life.

And then the ride Chad had taken her on—more muscles she'd never used before. Some were the same she'd used with Ladybird. Others, well, she hadn't known she had so many muscles.

She opened the door to the oversize shower and turned on the water. When it was good and hot, she stepped in. The water pelted her aching muscles, soothing them. She chose a bottle of shampoo—Mane 'n Tail? Trust Chad McCray to use horse shampoo—and squeezed some into her palm. As she massaged it into her scalp, she closed her eyes and inhaled the moist steam from the shower, clearing the dust from the night ride out of her nose. When her hair was thoroughly washed, she leaned back into the stream of water and let the shower rinse the lather away.

"Now that's about the most beautiful sight I've ever seen."

She opened her eyes and faced Chad, his gaze raking over her. She hadn't heard him open the shower door.

"Shut the door, Chad. You'll get the floor all wet."

"I have a maid, sugar."

"Go away, then. I need to wash."

"Not the right thing to say, sugar."

"What on earth are you talking about?"

"The right thing to say is, 'won't you join me, Chad?'"

"You want to take a shower with me?"

"More than I want my next meal, I think." He eyed her up and down. "I do believe I'm envious of those droplets of water meandering over your curves like that."

She giggled. "Well, you can't come in here like that."

"Like what?"

"With your clothes on, silly."

He chuckled. "I can take care of that quicker than a licorice whip."

"Licorice whip?"

Before she could give his saying another thought, his clothes were in a heap by the bathtub and he was in the shower with her, his body pressing to hers.

"Damn, what you do to me," he murmured, licking her earlobe.

His arousal grew against her stomach. She smiled to herself. He wanted her again. He picked her up and she wrapped her legs around her hips, clamping her mouth to his.

The kiss was as hungry as it had been last night. A full contact, wet-tongued, body-melting kiss. Catie couldn't get enough.

One of Chad's hands fumbled with the shower knob, and the water ceased to flow. He stepped out, still holding her, and dragged her to the bed.

"Chad? A towel?"

"Can't wait."

He fumbled in his nightstand and pulled out another condom.

"I thought you said we had to wait."

"Yeah, we should. But I can't. I don't seem to have any self-control when it comes to you, sugar." He looked her in the eye. "I can if you need me to. If you don't want this, I can go right back in that bathroom and take care of the problem myself."

"I—"

"It's okay, sugar."

"I... I want to do it again, Chad. I'm fine, really."

He touched between her legs and dipped one finger into her opening. She shivered.

"You're wet enough. Ready enough. You sure? Because I've gotta tell you, I want you so badly right now I can't think straight."

"Yes, it's okay. I want you."

He turned her around and pushed her onto the bed, so she was lying on her stomach. She heard the rip of the condom package, and then he was pulling her hips forward. The heat of his tongue laved her opening and his fingers slipped in. "That okay?"

She sighed. "God, yes. More than okay."

"Sugar, my God..." The tip of his erection nudged her flesh.

"Please..."

He plunged into her.

She cried out, but not from pain. From the pure unadulterated sweetness of the joining.

He stilled, and his body tensed behind her. He was worried. Worried that he'd hurt her again.

"It didn't hurt, Chad," she said. "It felt good. That's why I"—embarrassment flooded through her—"made that noise."

"Sweet heaven," he said, as he pulled out and thrust into her again.

Her hips moved backward, meeting him thrust for thrust.

"Catie, you're so beautiful." Chad's voice was rough, primal. "I wish you could see this, how I come into you. It's beautiful. Just beautiful."

She didn't need to see it. The beauty of the act melted her heart, opened her soul. Joining with him was a dream come true. Her skin began to tingle. "Chad—"

He reached under her and rubbed her swollen bud. "Yeah, sugar, yeah. Let yourself go. It's okay. Come. Come for me."

At the command of his words, she shattered as her climax exploded, her body soaring into euphoria.

"That's it. Make it feel good. So good." He continued to thrust into her. "Ah, I can feel you coming, baby. Coming all around me. So tight." He thrust hard one more time, so hard he pushed her down against the softness of the bed, his body covering hers. He kissed the back of her neck, her ear. "So good, sugar. Never this good with anyone else. Never."

He released her, lay down next to her, and pulled her into his embrace. Their slick bodies—wet from the shower, or from the perspiration from such joyful lovemaking?—melted together.

"What the hell have you done to me, Catie Bay?"

"I-I..." A tear trickled down her cheek. A tear for the sheer beauty of the experience they had just shared. Might share again. But wouldn't share forever.

"Hush. S'okay." He kissed her forehead. "Just let me hold you."

Catie breathed in the spicy masculine scent of Chad. She remembered the words he had spoken to her in the black of night, under the veil of sleep.

I've waited so long for you.

In a few moments, she drifted into slumber.

★ ★ ★

She awoke again when Chad's cell phone rang.

He disentangled himself from her and answered it. "Yeah?" Pause. "Okay, give me a few minutes."

He hung up and flung the phone onto his dresser. "Sugar, I need to go. They need me at one of the barns. A cow's gone into labor. Could you do me a favor and call Annie? Tell her to meet me at the south barn? She's number five on my speed dial." He pulled on a pair of jeans—no boxer briefs—and a clean pair of socks. Then he walked into the bathroom—to get his boots, she presumed.

Course he could have gotten one of the thirty-two pairs out of his closet. Catie smiled. Who'd have thought Chad McCray would have a thing for boots? Every fact she learned about him was a gift, a present she was unwrapping layer by layer. She had discovered some wonderful layers last night.

She hummed a happy tune under her breath.

As expected, he came out, boots on, and headed to the closet where he donned a denim shirt.

"Please, Catie?"

She jerked slightly. "What?"

"Call Annie? South barn?"

"Oh, yeah. Of course." She had been listening. Hadn't she?

"Never mind," he said, picking up his cell. "I need my phone with me. I'll call her on the way over. What I should do anyway. Don't know what I was thinking."

"I don't mind helping."

"I know, but I do this stuff by myself all the time." He grabbed his cell from the dresser and rushed toward the door. "Don't wait around. I'll likely be a while. I... Hell, I'll see you later, I guess."

And he was gone.

Nothing about when they might meet again. Nothing about hey, it was great. When can I see you? Let's go out sometime. How about a movie?

Nothing about the magic they had just shared.

And it *had* been magical. At least it had for her.

Catie's heart fell. Well, what had she expected? He'd made his position clear.

She decided to take another shower since the first one had been interrupted. Her hair was tangled again, this time wet, so she went to the bathroom and borrowed a brush she found on the counter. After combing out her snarls, she started the shower and entered, letting the hot water ease her tired body.

Unfortunately, it didn't do anything for her tired heart.

For that's what it was. Tired. Damn tired of loving Chad

McCray.

After a fifteen minute soak under the soothing showerhead, Catie dried off and found her clothes. She put on her jeans and bra, but had a quick thought. Chad wouldn't be back for a while yet, and she had a strange urge to put on one of his shirts. Just to feel it next to her skin, as if she really belonged to him, lived in this room with him. Was his woman.

She chose a white cotton with pearl snaps. It hung on her, but when she inhaled the clean crispiness of it, she felt like she'd come home.

She walked out of the bedroom and decided to look around the house. Huge, as she'd realized last night, but in broad daylight, the Colorado sun streaming through the windows, it was gigantic. She walked through the living room, the dining room, all the time fantasizing about being mistress of this manor, showing guests in, smiling and laughing, Chad by her side, his arm draped possessively around her shoulders. She waltzed into the shiny kitchen and imagined preparing a hearty ranch breakfast for Chad and their children, shuffling them off to school, and then going about her daily chores. Chad would come home at noon for a hot lunch she'd prepare, and then, before he went back to work, he'd take her to the bedroom and love her because he couldn't wait until the evening.

Yeah, that's how it would be.

She shook her head. Damn, Chad was right. She was a silly little kid. Playing house like a schoolgirl.

She headed back to the bedroom and replaced Chad's shirt in his closet.

How was she going to get home?

Chad had brought her on Eclipse, and the walk back to her house was ten miles at least. She sighed as she slipped into her own shirt.

A piece of garbage caught her eye by the wastebasket, and she reached to pick it up. Chad's condom.

Her heart skidded to a stop.

There was a tear in it.

CHAPTER EIGHT

Driving to the south barn, Chad called Annie and then swore to himself as he pushed his cell phone back into his pocket.

What the hell had he been thinking, asking Catie to call the vet? As if he'd never had a calf birthing before. He'd always called the damn vet himself. He didn't need someone else to do it. She wasn't his helpmate. It wasn't her problem.

He shook his head.

The whole damn night had been a mistake. But oh, how her tight little body had sheathed him. He'd barely gotten into her and she'd gripped him like a vise. He'd had to work to keep from coming then and there. Now, all he could think about was burying himself in her sweetness again.

A spike of heat hit him low in the gut, and his groin tightened in expectation.

Not a boner. Not now.

Christ.

All he had to do was imagine her pretty face, her sweet raspberry kisses, her lovely brick-orange nipples.

The tangy scent of her heated sex.

He was a goner.

Like he always said about his brothers. Always said they were goners. Damn.

This had to stop, and it had to stop now.

Otherwise he'd break her heart, and he wasn't sure he could live with himself if he did that.

She wasn't in love with him. This was a little girl crush that had gotten out of hand, yes, but it was nothing more than pure infatuation. He'd help her see that. He shook his head slowly. He sure couldn't help her see that if he was sleeping with her.

Yep, it had to stop.

Goddamn it.

Raspberries were his favorite fruit.

★ ★ ★

When Chad didn't return within the hour, Catie called her sister, Angie, to pick her up.

Angie, the gossip of all gossips, flooded her with questions of why her baby sister was at Chad McCray's house. Catie fended off the inquiries as best she could. They'd gone riding. It had been late, and they were closer to his house. She'd stayed in one of his guest rooms.

Luckily, it didn't occur to her sister to ask why she wasn't riding Ladybird home. She didn't want to talk about this to Angie or to anyone. Not now. Not ever. She was too busy ruminating about the torn condom.

What would happen? Chad didn't want to get married. If he didn't want to get married, he sure didn't want kids.

Now sitting back in her bedroom, Catie's tummy tumbled and threatened to empty, even though she hadn't eaten since the party. Her mind was a whirl of conflicting thoughts. A baby? She wasn't sure she was ready for a baby. But a sweet little boy or girl who looked just like his handsome daddy? Oh, she could make do.

But Chad? What would Chad say? Would he marry her?

Would he want to? Would he want the baby? She choked back a sob. She might be alone in this. She would never abandon her baby, but could she raise a child alone? Women did it every day. She was certainly as capable as anyone else.

She forced her thoughts to the back of her mind. This was all purely speculation. Not everyone who had unprotected sex got pregnant. Couples all over the world spent all kinds of time and money trying to get pregnant. Chances were good that nothing would happen. What were the statistics? Like eleven percent chance of pregnancy from one unprotected encounter? Still pretty good odds. And the condom might have ripped when Chad took it off.

There, she felt better. Nothing to worry about. At least not yet.

For now, she had a rodeo queen competition to win.

"Angie!" she called.

Her sister arrived, breathless. "Yeah? I was just on my way out."

"I'm entering the rodeo queen thing."

"You?"

"Yeah, me. What's your problem?"

Angie, who was Chad's age, had been crowned rodeo queen fourteen years earlier, at the ripe age of eighteen. Bakersville's youngest rodeo queen ever.

"Aren't you too old?"

"Nope. Not too old. And you're gonna help me win."

"If this is just a ploy to get Chad McCray to notice you, I want no part of it."

Damn. Was she that transparent?

"I can ride circles around you, and you won."

"There's more to it than just riding, and you know it.

You'll need to dress the part. You'll actually have to wear makeup, little tomboy."

"I wore make up last night, didn't I?"

"Barely."

"Just 'cause I don't apply it with a putty knife—"

"Uh, little sis, if you want my help, I'd stop with the insults."

"Yeah, yeah." Catie nodded. "You're right. Okay." She grinned. "You have to help me, Angie. I need you. I intend to win this stupid thing."

"That's just my point, Catie. If you think it's a stupid thing, you have no business entering."

"You're right," Catie agreed. "It's worthy, actually. It showcases the equestrian talents of Bakersville's young women, right?"

"Yes, among other things."

"Like?"

"Poise, intelligence, beauty, to name a few."

"I've got those."

"I'll give you beauty and intelligence, Cate, but poise? Sweetie, you trip over your own two feet."

Catie cringed. She hadn't thought of her perpetual clumsiness. "Well, I'll have to get over that, won't I? Besides, no one can beat me on horseback. Isn't that most of what this competition is about?"

"Don't kid yourself, sweetie. It's a beauty contest, pure and simple."

"No. No, it's not. I mean, the McCray brothers are judging it. Two of them are married. What interest would they have in a beauty contest?"

"Little bit, you are so naïve." Angelina laughed and shook

her head. "But if you're bound and determined to enter, I think I can work with you. You'll need to work hard with Ladybird. You've been gone awhile."

"You make it sound like I've been in hibernation for four years. I did manage to ride a horse or two in Europe. They have them there, you know."

"All right, all right. Simmer down, little bit."

"I think I've outgrown that nickname, Angie."

"Okay, Catie. We'll need to think about your wardrobe, and your platform."

"Platform? This is rodeo queen, not Miss U.S.A."

"Still, you need to stand for something."

"I stand for the rodeo. For the art of the equestrienne."

"Hmm. That might work."

"It's gotta work. It's all I've got."

"We'll work with it. We'll take this competition back to what it's really about. The horsewoman. Rodeo. Hmm, it's too bad you never stuck with barrel racing. We could get Dusty to give you some pointers."

"Angie, I'm not going to become a champion barrel racer in a week."

"True. You'll be able to do the required patterns though." Angie paused. "You'll do, little bit. You'll do just fine."

Though she cringed again at little bit, Catie welcomed her sister's expertise. God knew she'd need it.

★ ★ ★

Chad was glad to have Annie at the birth. The calf had had to be turned, and Chad hated doing that. His hands and forearms were big and caused needless pain to the cow. Annie took care of it, and the calf was born quickly and was already standing and searching for a teat.

"Thanks, Annie," he said at the house, while they were washing up.

"It's my job. No need to thank me."

"Yeah, yeah. I know. But thanks anyway."

"You're welcome. I need to get back, though. Dallas has a meeting later today and I need to be there for the girls."

"You can bring 'em over here if you've got something to do."

Annie smiled. "Don't you have a ranch to run?"

"Yeah, but heck, I love spending time with them. You know I'll take 'em anytime."

"Well..." Annie hedged a bit. "If you could, it'd help me out. I promised Catie I'd get together with her and help her prepare for this rodeo queen thing."

"You?"

"Don't look so surprised. I won a pageant or two in my day."

"You're kidding."

She swatted him with the towel she'd used to dry her hands. "Thanks a lot."

"Nah, I didn't mean it like that. You know I think you're beautiful. Hell, if my brother hadn't snatched you up—"

"Then you wouldn't have either, Chad. The day you settle down'll be a day of celebration for sure."

He lifted his lips in his trademark lazy smile. "Won't be anytime soon, Doc. Tell me though, because I'm morbidly curious. What's your experience with pageants?"

"It's every little girl's dream to be Miss America, isn't it? Especially a girl who grew up in Atlantic City?"

"Maybe, but I'd've bet money it was never yours."

She guffawed. "Okay, you got me. It wasn't mine. It was my ma's. She took me through several local pageants when I was a teen, and I'm embarrassed to say, I did pretty well until I was old enough to enter the regional pageants."

"What happened then?"

"I had the looks, the poise, they all said. But the bigger pageants have talent competitions, and I didn't have a speck of it. I can't carry a tune, never took to an instrument, I look like a marionette when I dance." She laughed. "You can't get up on stage and perform a dissection on a fetal pig. That's the stuff I was good at."

"Well, there's no talent competition for rodeo queen. It's just struttin' around and making a stupid ass speech. There's a little horsemanship involved, but it's stuff Catie can do in her sleep. It ain't no Miss America, Annie."

"She wants to do it, Chad. Quit giving her guff." Annie wiped her hands once more and replaced the towel. "Besides, I can't imagine you or any other guy in Bakersville having a problem watching Catie strut her stuff in a bikini."

"Sure. Yeah." Chad nodded, but his gut hurt like a knife had stabbed it.

He sure as hell didn't want Catie strutting her stuff for anyone but him.

And that fact gnawed at the back of his neck like a persistent mosquito.

CHAPTER NINE

Dear Miss Bay:

We welcome you to the Bakersville Rodeo Queen competition. Enclosed please find your agenda for the week, rules and regulations, and horsemanship patterns. We are looking forward to having you join us for this week of fun and fellowship honoring the traditions of the Bakersville Rodeo.

Who is the Bakersville Rodeo Queen? She is a young woman who wishes to be a leader in her community. She loves horses and the western way of life. She will represent the Bakersville Rodeo during the year of her reign and will also represent the town in other community activities. She portrays excellent sportsmanship, high moral character, and careful and humane treatment of animals. She must understand the sport of Rodeo in its entirety and be able to explain any part of Rodeo to onlookers. She must speak intelligently and with dignity. Although this is not a beauty pageant, the Bakersville Rodeo Queen should act, speak, and dress according to the prestige this title represents.

You must ride the same horse all week and have current health papers and a negative Coggins test on the animal.

Please read your agenda carefully. Be sure to contact the competition coordinator with your platform and a description of your outfit and swimwear for Wednesday night's party so the emcee can prepare his dialogue for the fashion show. Your entry fee includes one guest entry for the luncheon on Saturday. You're required to give a three to five minute speech on the subject of *your platform at the luncheon. If you would like to bring extra guests, please contact the coordinator. Tickets are $35.00.*

Please forward a five by seven photo of yourself in western attire to the pageant coordinator.

If you have any questions, please feel free to contact the coordinator.

We look forward to having you in the competition.

Sincerely,

Dallas J. McCray, Judge

Zachary B. McCray, Judge

Charles M. McCray, Judge

Judy Williamson, Competition Coordinator

Chad's name was Charles? Catie smiled. She never knew.

Not a beauty pageant? She scoffed. Right. What was the swimwear modeling for?

She read the letter—which had arrived via special messenger, due, no doubt to her late entry into the contest—again. She'd have to have Annie do a Coggins on Ladybird to make sure the horse was free of equine infectious anemia. She wasn't sure she had record of the last one.

A three to five minute speech on her platform? She chuckled. She could talk all year about horses. Narrowing it down would be the difficulty.

Judy Williamson. The owner of the salon where Amber worked. Would that give Amber an in? She laughed out loud. No more than sleeping with Chad McCray would give her an in. In fact, she'd better keep that little tidbit quiet or she might be disqualified.

Not too much of a problem. She'd left his house Sunday morning. Here it was Tuesday, and he'd made no attempt to see her.

Catie put the letter aside and looked at the agenda. The party and fashion show was tomorrow night! And she had to call Judy with a description of her outfits. *Help!* And she'd need a photo of herself, too. Quickly!

Annie'd be busy all day, and Dusty wasn't much of a fashion expert. But Catie's big sister, Angie, was. She'd get Angie to take her shopping today. Maybe they'd drive to Denver, even.

Friday evening was the horsemanship event. Catie glanced at the patterns. *Yes!* She and Ladybird would have no difficulty. She giggled, wondering if Amber and her acrylic nails had ever been on a horse.

Saturday was the big day. The luncheon was at noon, during which Catie would make her speech. Afterward, each contestant would have a personal interview with the judges.

She froze.

A personal interview with Chad. How would she face him? Zach and Dallas would be there, too, but still...

She read on. She'd ride in the Grand Entry that evening, with introductions and crowning at 7:30 p.m., before the rodeo events started. On Sunday, there'd be a parade, and the new rodeo queen would lead it.

Okay. She could do this.

She scanned the rules and regulations quickly.

Yeah, yeah. The age limit, eighteen to twenty-two. The horse papers and Coggins test. No stallions. Conduct yourself properly. Jeans and a long sleeve western blouse for the horsemanship. No gloves or chaps.

Rule number ten stared out at her, as though mocking her.

The winner of the Bakersville Rodeo Queen competition

agrees not to marry during the year of her reign. If she should marry, the title will go to the first runner-up.

She sighed. Not a problem. The only man she wanted to marry had no interest in marrying her. Done deal. She could be the rodeo queen.

★ ★ ★

Wednesday evening came before Catie felt ready. As she waited for her turn to model her western wear, she stared at the other contestants. They all looked more elegant than she did. What had she been thinking? Chad was right. She was just a kid. A kid trying to act like a grown-up. Didn't matter that most of these contestants were younger than she was. They'd started preparing months ago.

"You're up next, Caitlyn," Amber said, rubbing her shoulder. "Then me. I'm so nervous."

Amber looked beautiful in a black satin western shirt and white leather jeans. Catie felt infantile next to her, wearing the studded red shirt she'd chosen. She'd decided against the leather jeans and wore black denim. Angie had tried to talk her into leather, but Catie hated the way it felt against her skin. Sticky and stifling in the summer heat. But her red ostrich boots looked good, and her red-and-black studded belt.

"Caitlyn Bay!" Judy called.

"Go." Amber nudged her. "And good luck."

"Yeah, you too," Catie said, trying not to hurl.

She walked out to the makeshift runway that had been set up in the arena.

The emcee's deep voice began. "Next up is Bakersville's own Caitlyn Bay."

HELEN HARDT

Catie wished she'd taken Annie's advice about Vaseline on her teeth. Her lips stuck to her gums. "Caitlyn is twenty-one years old and recently returned to Bakersville after studying at the Sorbonne in Paris for four years. We're glad to have her back. She's the daughter of Wayne and Maria Bay of Cha Cha Ranch.

"Caitlyn is wearing a Nash western shirt of crimson silk accented with silver studs."

Catie turned, sticking her hips out and her shoulders back, as Annie had taught her. Hoping like hell she didn't look like a complete moron.

"Caitlyn's studded leather belt is also by Nash, and her boot cut black denims are by Levi Strauss. She sports gold-tipped red ostrich boots by Anderson Bean. Thank you, Caitlyn."

Catie smiled to the crowd, and then, as Annie had taught her, met each judge's eyes. Her breath caught when Chad's dark gaze converged with hers. His eyes burned into her. Zach and Dallas were busy writing, but Chad's eyes never left her. She whipped her head around, but her ankle wobbled. She caught herself and walked off the stage.

"Next up is Amber Cross," the emcee said.

Catie rushed to her makeshift dressing room and sat down, breathing heavily. She'd done everything Annie said. She'd made eye contact with the judges, and it had damn near taken her out of the competition.

How the hell was she going to do it in the freaking bikini she had to put on?

The bikini had been Angie's idea. Catie had wanted to go for a maillot.

"You've got the bod, sweetie," Angie had said. "Use it to

your advantage."

Yeah, she was really going to hurl.

Her hands shaking, she stripped out of her western outfit and dressed in the bikini. Had it been this tiny in the store yesterday?

Why did she want to do this again?

She tied the silky cover-up over her hips and waited for Judy to call her.

It happened what seemed like only seconds later.

"Catie Bay! You're up."

She took a deep breath and swallowed, hoping she wouldn't trip in the black stilettos Angie had insisted upon. She spied Amber in a red thong bikini. God. Angie had wanted to go thong, but Catie had put her foot down. Angie had wanted to go red, too. No way. Wearing a red sundress to a family party was one thing, another thing altogether to strut around in a candy-apple-red bikini.

"Here's Bakersville's own Caitlyn Bay again, wearing a sea-green bikini by Lenny."

Catie smiled as she walked outward. The crowd cheered. Had they cheered that loudly when she'd worn her western wear? She wasn't sure.

"The bandeau top features a malachite adornment in the center and is fully lined. The American bottom—"

Catie inhaled and untied the cover up, flipping it behind her shoulder. Again she stuck out her hips.

"—features soft construction sides for a smooth and flattering fit." He cleared his throat. "It provides moderate coverage in the back." Catie turned around.

She walked down the platform and again made eye contact with Dallas, and then Zach. She swallowed, gulped in a quick breath, and turned up her lips in what she hoped was a dazzling smile. She met Chad's gaze.

His mouth had dropped, and he looked like he'd been knocked into a cocked hat.

★ ★ ★

"Tough call," Zach said, after all the contestants had finished modeling.

"Not too tough," Dallas drawled. "I know who my pick is."

"Me too," Zach agreed. "How about you, Chad?"

Chad hadn't breathed since Catie left the stage. He wasn't sure who had come next, or how many. The image of her gorgeous breasts covered by that strip of sea-green silk burned into his mind. All he could think about was ripping the thing off her and clamping his mouth onto one of her sweet nipples. And that moderate covering bottom had done more for him than all the thongs he'd seen. Hell, he knew the precious treasure that silk covered. "Don't know. They were all pretty."

Zach grinned. "Didn't you think there was one who stood out?"

"Like I said"—he cleared his throat—"I don't know."

"Well, you'd better make a decision," Dallas said. "You have to rate them."

Chad choked. The thought of his older brothers—of any other men, and there were plenty in the audience—seeing Catie in that sexy getup was more than his heart—and another stubborn part of his anatomy—could take. His jeans were so tight right now, he thought he might burst.

"This is stupid," he said, and hurriedly scribbled random

numbers next to each of the contestants' names. When he got to Catie, he couldn't help himself.

He gave her a twelve.

The top score was ten.

★ ★ ★

Catie put the cover-up back on for the party. Stupid tradition dictated that the competitors wear their swimwear to the outdoor festivities held poolside at the hotel. She'd tossed the stilettos and was wandering around in bare feet. The light pink toenail polish Angie had applied made her feel conspicuous, but Amber had fire-engine red on, so Catie decided she was being silly. She chatted with some of the other contestants and a few friends from town. The spread was fabulous, but she couldn't eat. She was still fighting nausea from her nerves. She felt naked. Like she was having one of those naked dreams when she was a kid. Didn't make sense. All the other girls were dressed just as she was, many more skimpily.

Still, goose bumps erupted on her flesh, despite the heat.

This wasn't really her.

But she'd gotten into this, and she was determined to see it through.

When the McCray brothers arrived, the contestants flocked to them, offering to freshen their drinks, their plates, kiss their muscular asses... Well, not quite.

Catie thought she might hurl again.

Amber, of course, hung all over Chad. Was it possible he'd taken her to bed since they'd been together?

Catie's heart fell at the thought. No. He wouldn't do that, if for no other reason than it would be unethical to bed one of the contestants when he was a judge.

Of course, it hadn't stopped him from bedding her, which meant he really hadn't believed she'd enter. No one thought she'd go through with it.

He hadn't contacted her at all. She sighed. He'd made it quite clear they had no future. And she had accepted it. At least she thought she had. At the time, it had seemed a small price to pay to be loved by him once.

How was she to know that once with Chad McCray would never be enough?

"Hey, you looked gorgeous."

Catie turned and faced Annie's pretty face. "Oh, thanks. I couldn't have done it without your tips. Or Angie's fashion advice." She crossed her arms over her chest. "I feel like a deer caught in headlights, Annie. How do those other girls walk around nearly naked without a constant blush on their faces? I don't get it."

"Yeah, I never liked the swimsuit part of pageantry either," Annie agreed. "But you have to admit it tests your poise. It's not easy strutting your stuff dressed in next to nothing."

"No kidding. So, did I..."

"Did you what?"

"Did I look poised? I mean, I was fighting back puke the whole time, Annie, and I should have taken your advice about the Vaseline. My lips stuck to my teeth something awful."

Annie laughed in her boisterous way. "You looked beautiful, hon. Just gorgeous. And I didn't notice anything off about your smile. You did a great job of holding the contents of your belly in. Every man around me couldn't take his eyes off you. The women either, for that matter."

"I just never thought of myself as pageant material."

"I know. Neither did I, but I did okay. And so can you."

"You still can, Annie. Your exotic looks are timeless."

"Hon, I'm an old married woman of thirty-four with two babies."

"There are scads of pageants for older women."

"Not for me." She laughed. "But I appreciate the compliment. You, however, are young enough to make a go of this. You've got the height, the looks, the poise. You were absolutely amazing out there. You're going to win this thing, Catie."

"Well, if I win this one, it'll be because of my horsemanship and equestrian knowledge. Not how good I look in a bikini," she said flatly. "I can ride circles around these other girls."

"I've no doubt of that," Annie said. "With the McCray boys judging, they'll put lots of stock in the horse part, much more than the bikini part." She winked. "Except maybe for the youngest."

Catie warmed under her friend's violet gaze. "Yeah, he does love the ladies," she said wistfully.

"That he does, hon," Annie said. "But make no mistake about it, you've caught his eye."

"He thinks I'm a kid."

"I'd bet he doesn't think that anymore. Anyone who saw you modeling that bikini tonight couldn't possibly think you were a kid. You're a grown woman, Catie. You've lived abroad. You've seen the world. You've still got a lot to learn, but no one can call you a kid anymore."

"Chad can."

"Chad'll see the light of day. Don't you worry."

Catie rolled her eyes. "How can he see the light of day

with Amber and her thong blocking his view?"

Annie laughed. "Haven't you noticed?"

"Noticed what?"

"Amber and her thong may be hanging on his arm. And those other girls might be fetching his drinks, wiggling their boobs and their butts in his face, but his eyes haven't left you since we got here."

Catie's heart lurched, and she looked behind her shoulder to Chad. Sure enough, she caught his gaze. He looked away.

"Maybe you ought to go offer to get him something."

"And play those silly games? I'd rather be hung by my toenails from barbed wire."

"Silly games they may be, but do you want some other woman to get her claws in your man?"

"My man?"

"Hell, yes, your man. Fight for him, hon. He wants you. He just doesn't know it yet."

Oh, he knows it, Catie thought. Physically, at least. Emotionally, though... That was the key. He needed to fall in love with her, as she had with him. And Annie *did* have a point. She was wasting a valuable opportunity to get close to him.

"All right, Annie. If you'll excuse me."

Catie turned and marched straight toward Chad McCray and his harem. So focused was her gaze, so focused her concentration, that she didn't see the waiter wheeling a cart full of food perpendicular to her until it was too late. She lost her footing and landed in the hotel pool.

The scream lodged in her throat erupted just as the liquid covered her face, causing her to gulp in a mouthful of the chlorinated water. Instinctively, she breathed in through her nose, and though she had been a champion swimmer in high school, she found herself floundering in the five-feet-deep pool. What a clumsy idiot.

A strong hand steadied her. "You okay?" A deep voice said.

She coughed and looked into the handsome face of Joe Bradley, the town mechanic.

"Yeah, I think so," she sputtered.

Joe's gaze dropped to her chest. What? She looked down and gasped. Her bandeau bikini top was gone!

Why had she listened to Angie and gone strapless? Was it around her waist? No. A strip of sea green floated on the bottom of the pool, away from her.

This could only happen to Catie Bay. The girl who tripped over her own two feet daily. The girl who was brilliant on horseback, but a calamity on her own legs.

She crushed her arms around her chest.

"Get away from her, Bradley!" came Chad's voice. He stood at the edge of the pool and stripped off his western shirt. His golden chest gleamed in the setting sun. "Come on, Catie," he said. "I've got you."

"Chad, I can't."

"Sure you can. Just come over here to the ladder and step out. I'll get you covered. Don't worry."

Snickers and catcalls cut through the haze of Catie's thoughts. She was waterlogged. She couldn't see, couldn't think. She tightened her arms around her chest. Her breasts weren't huge, but they were big enough that her arms wouldn't cover them all the way. A bronze nipple peeked out, pebbled from the cold water.

"I think I know who's gonna win that contest!" A voice shouted.

"Shut the fuck up!" Chad said. "Leave her alone." He turned back to Catie. "Come on, I got you."

In her haze, she walked to the ladder, still coughing from the pool water. As soon as her chest left the water, Chad had her covered with his shirt. "Come on, sugar. Let's get you dried off."

"Ch-Chad." Her teeth chattered, and she wondered why. She wasn't cold. Nerves. Had to be nerves. The laughter and jeering met her ears with force. All eyes were on her. She must be turning thirteen shades of crimson.

"What?"

"It was an accident."

He chuckled, the warmth of his arm around her shoulders a comfort. "I know that."

"I just didn't want you to think—"

"That you'd orchestrate a stunt like that to get attention? To help win the contest?" He shook his head as they entered the hotel.

The air-conditioning hit Catie with a snap. Now she shivered even more.

"Some of those girls might try something like that, but not you. You've got too much class. Don't think I didn't notice how you tried your damnedest to stay away from Zach, Dallas, and me, while most of the other contestants were falling all over themselves to serve us. That doesn't hold water with me. Or with Zach and Dallas. We'll pick our winner based on merit. Fair and square."

"Oh. Yeah, I know you will." Her teeth chattered again. She'd grind them down to stubs if this kept up.

"Come on, let's get you taken care of." He headed toward the elevators, dragging her along.

"Where are we going?"

"My room."

"You have a room here?"

"Yeah. I decided to stay in town tonight. In case I imbibed a little too much at the party." He pushed the button. "Tenth floor."

"But...I need my clothes."

"Are they in your car? I'll have the bellhop get them."

"Uh, yeah. Yeah, that'd be fine."

"I'll make sure someone gets your bikini top, too."

She scoffed. "Really, I couldn't care less. I doubt I'll ever wear the thing again."

"Now sugar, for you not to wear that thing again would be a crime against nature. You sure looked pretty."

Her body heated with his words.

"Course you look prettier without it." The elevator doors closed, and Chad opened his shirt and burned his gaze onto her breasts. Heat blazed on her body, especially between her legs.

"You are so damn beautiful, Catie. I couldn't keep my eyes off you when you were strutting on that stage. I wanted to punch both my brothers right there for looking at you."

"They weren't looking at me."

"The hell they weren't. They may be happily married, but they appreciate a beautiful woman as much as the next man does. In fact, I wanted to punch every man there. No man should get to see you like that."

"It's beachwear, Chad. Women wear it all the time."

"Not my woman."

Catie's heart lurched. Had she heard correctly? He hadn't just referred to her as "his woman," had he? She thought about asking, but didn't dare. He might take it back. She sighed. He probably didn't even realize he'd said it.

Chad closed the shirt when the elevator reached its destination. The hall was vacant, thank God. She didn't need anyone seeing her going into Chad's room. That couldn't possibly look good for the competition. Though not explicitly stated in the rules, fraternizing with a judge had to be against pageant regulations.

"Go on in the bathroom and dry off," Chad said. "I'll call downstairs and have your clothes brought up. What's your car make and license number?"

"It's a green Accord, with"—she hesitated—"Catie Bug vanity plates." She warmed with embarrassment. "I need to get that changed."

Chad chuckled as he picked up the hotel phone. Catie headed to the bathroom. Afraid to look in the mirror, she went straight to the shower. She hated chlorine on her skin. It made her itch like the dickens. A shower was her only option. She turned it on and the water left the showerhead with a whoosh. Once the room was good and steamy, she stepped inside.

This was Bakersville's finest hotel—which wasn't saying much. The shampoo was cheap and runny, but she made do. After lathering her head twice, she rinsed it out and smoothed on the equally unimpressive conditioner. While she let it soak in, she lathered her body and got rid of the wretched chlorine.

Chad knocked on the door and then entered. "Damn, sugar, what'd you get in the shower for? You tryin' to tempt me with candy?"

"I hate chlorine on my skin, Chad. Get out of here!"

"I had to go down and get your clothes myself. The bellhops were all busy. All two of them." He laughed. But he didn't leave the room.

"I said go on, now," Catie said.

"Hmm. This is quite a dilemma, isn't it? I'm thinking I might need a shower myself. I've been knee deep in this pageant bullshit since sunup. Got hands runnin' the ranch."

"Yeah. If you haven't been ranching, you don't need a shower. Get out!"

"I've already got my shirt off..." Chad pulled off his boots and socks and unbuckled his jeans. "Don't know whether I can trust you alone in the shower, anyway. Never took you for such a klutz, falling into the pool in the middle of a party. Can't imagine what might happen to you on a slippery shower floor." All the while his lazy grin lit up his handsome face. "Seems like we have some unfinished business in a shower."

"Chad...no. It's unethical. I'm a contestant. You're a judge."

"You'll just have to disqualify yourself."

He pulled down his jeans and boxers, leaving them in a heap. His arousal sprang forward, and Catie widened her eyes. Still gorgeous. Still huge. Still all for her.

He opened the shower door and joined her, crushing her to his hard muscular body. "Damn, you feel good, sugar."

"Chad..."

His mouth clamped onto hers, and she was lost. The kiss fired her blood like nothing had before. His tongue tangled with hers, tasting, devouring, until she had to rip her mouth away to breathe. Embers smoldered between her legs. Chad gripped her breasts as he sucked on her neck, her shoulders.

"I need you."

Need? He needed her? He hadn't said he wanted her. He said he needed her. That had to be a good thing, right?

HELEN HARDT

He picked her up and she wrapped her legs around his hips, meeting his mouth again. The head of his shaft teased her entrance. Then, "Damn."

"What?"

"Forgot the condom."

"Oh."

For a moment, Catie remembered the torn condom in Chad's bedroom. She'd been so busy readying for the pageant, she hadn't thought about that in days.

They were absolutely not having sex without a condom. She removed her legs from his hips and slid down his body.

In fact, they weren't having sex, period. It would be unethical, and they had already engaged in behavior unbefitting a contestant and a judge. She needed to get dressed and leave.

Now.

If she didn't, she'd fall right into bed with him—God, how she wanted to fall into bed with him—but Catie Bay was a good girl. She followed the rules.

Well, sort of.

She needed to get into her clothes and get back down to the party before anyone realized how long she and Chad had been gone together.

She pushed him away and left the shower stall, grabbing a towel and wrapping it around her dripping body.

"Sugar, I can pull out."

"This isn't happening, Chad. It's unethical."

"It's not like we've never done this before."

"Before I wasn't an official contestant. I am now, and this is unethical." She dried off quickly with a soft hotel towel and wrapped her hair in another, trying to ignore her racing pulse, the flutter between her legs. "I'm getting dressed, and I'm rejoining the party. I suggest you do the same."

"You're right. I'm sorry I put you in this position. I should know better."

Chad left the stall and dried off, deliberately, or so it seemed to Catie, wiggling his gorgeously-formed ass in her face.

"I've already lost points for my clumsiness at falling into that damn pool, and I—"

"You haven't lost any points. Zach and Dallas won't hold that against you."

"I was in the middle of a sentence, Chad."

"Sorry," he chuckled, "ma'am."

"So they won't hold it against me. What about you?" She stared straight into his long lashed eyes.

"Sugar, there are tons of things I'd love to hold against you." He moved toward her, his body dripping, but she wriggled out of his reach. "Tripping into the pool ain't one of them."

Catie took a deep breath, trying not to stare at his powerful thighs, the dark hair matted down by water. "I need to borrow your hairbrush." Without waiting for an answer, she rummaged through his shaving bag and pulled out a brush. She brushed her hair quickly and fluffed it with her fingers. It would have to air dry. She pinched her cheeks and then left the bathroom to put on her clothes.

A few minutes later, she was clad in her black denims, red shirt, and ostrich boots. Much better than the bikini. Chad hadn't left the bathroom. She had left the bikini bottom in the bathroom. Well, no harm done. She'd rather not see the damn thing again, anyway.

She left the room, closed the door behind her, and thudded

back against it for a moment, her heart thundering.

She'd had the chance to make love with Chad again, and she had blown it.

For a stupid pageant she really had no interest in winning.

CHAPTER TEN

That beautiful woman had walked away from him.

Chad switched the shower to lukewarm—he never could take a cold shower—and slid down the cold tile to sit on the floor. The water pelted his body.

He wasn't going to just get over her. This was insanity, plain and simple.

He'd been worried his ultimate rejection would hurt her. Her and her schoolgirl crush.

He'd never dreamed she might reject *him*.

Was that a little bit of pain he felt in his heart? Nah, couldn't be.

She was just another beautiful woman, right? Beautiful women were a dime a dozen, and right now there were at least a dozen down at the party waiting to fawn all over him. Might as well take advantage of it. Even if the one he wanted was bound and determined to do the ethical thing.

He respected her for that. Caitlyn Bay was all class. All elegance and inner, as well as outer, beauty. Part of him was glad she'd stopped him, because all heaven knew he couldn't have stopped himself. He was a judge, after all, and she was a contestant.

Chad stood, rinsed off, and turned off the water. Time to get back to business.

He dressed and returned to the party, but Catie was gone. Amber hung onto him, and she sure was pretty. Her pert little bottom looked darn nice in that red thong.

"Sweetheart," he said, "how'd you like to have a drink?"

"You're crazy," Amber said. "Now you want to be with me?"

"Sure." He trailed his finger over her shoulder lightly. Funny, none of the sparks he felt when he touched Catie. Still, her skin was warm and soft, and imagining his lips sliding over it was a pleasant image indeed. "Come on, honey. This party's dying down anyway. Let's go. I'm not suggesting anything improper, just a drink."

Amber swatted his hand away from her face. "Are you trying to get me disqualified?"

"Huh?"

"You think I can't see where this is headed? You sleep with me, and I'm thrown out of the rodeo queen competition. You're nuts. I've worked too hard for this."

"Aw, hell, Amber, you only signed up last week, same as Catie."

"Well, it means just as much to me as it does to Catie. You'd like that, wouldn't you?"

"Like what?"

"You'd like to sleep with me and have me disqualified, so your precious Catie can win."

"My precious Catie? What the hell are you talkin' about? I was suggesting you and I have a drink together. Nothing more."

"You haven't taken your eyes off her all night. The other girls and I, we've noticed."

"Amber, I'm not the only judge."

"Surely you have some influence over your brothers."

Chad couldn't help the boisterous guffaw that flew from

his throat. "Honey, I have about as much control over those two as a fly has over a spider. I'm the baby of the family, and they never let me forget it."

"Still, I'll have to pass."

"Fine. Fine." Chad rolled his eyes. Amber didn't stoke his fire anyway. He'd truly only wanted some company, not a fuck. There was only one woman he wanted to take to his bed.

He hadn't yet had enough of Catie Bay.

What the hell he was going to do about that?

★ ★ ★

Two days later, Catie and Ladybird waited their turn at the patterns. Amber had already competed, and Catie had been surprised to see that the other woman actually knew her way around a horse. She'd watched with fascination as Amber flawlessly ran the patterns. Amber hailed from San Antonio, so Catie shouldn't have been surprised. Her horse was a beauty, too—a creamy white Appaloosa mare with brown spots.

But no horse could compare to Ladybird. Ladybird was pure chocolate all over, even her mane and tail. Catie had curried her to a fine shine and had her re-shod a few days prior. She and Ladybird understood each other even though four years had passed since they'd worked together regularly. Once in her saddle, Catie felt she'd never left. Comfy, cozy, and perfect.

When the emcee called her name, she and Ladybird nailed each pattern to perfection. They moved fluidly, as though they were one.

She smiled at the deafening applause from the stands in the arena.

She waved to the spectators, and they cheered even louder. She wouldn't know her scores until the competition was over the next evening, but that didn't matter. She'd be at the top of the heap when it came to horsemanship.

She and Ladybird walked past the judge's table, and again, she made eye contact with each one. She gave Chad an extra-large smile.

★ ★ ★

Catie sweated bullets as she waited in the hall in front of the hotel conference room for her turn to be interviewed by the three judges. Her speech had gone well, if she said so herself. Amber had already had her interview and had wished Catie luck before she left to get ready for the final presentation later, before the start of Saturday night's rodeo festivities.

"It's not too bad," Amber had said. "They didn't grill me or anything. Just lots of questions about horses and the rodeo."

Catie had thanked Amber and given her a quick hug. Amber hadn't had to tell Catie about the interview. After all, they were competitors. It was a nice gesture, and one Catie wouldn't forget. She and Amber might be friends after all.

Patti Sherberg came out of the room nibbling on her lower lip.

"How'd it go, Patti?" Catie asked.

"Okay, I guess. Watch out for the oldest one. Dallas. He asks some hard questions. If you ask me, he's taking this all much too serious."

"What about the others?"

"They weren't quite so bad," Patti laughed shakily. "But I was a bundle of nerves. I felt like I was talking way too fast, not making any sense."

"Everyone loses points for nerves."

"You don't. Your patterns were perfect, Catie. You'll win for sure."

"I don't lose points for nerves?" Catie laughed. "Who was it that fell into the pool and lost her top Wednesday night? Now simmer down. I'm sure you did fine."

Patti nodded and walked away, her shoulders slumping.

The door to the conference room opened, and Dallas McCray's handsome head peeked out. "You can come in now, Catie."

"Thank you."

She walked in, and Dallas sat down at a table with Zach and Chad.

"Have a seat," he said.

"Thank you."

Geez. She'd already said that. No time to get all jumbled up now.

"It's great to have you back in town, Catie," Zach said. "So why don't you tell us why you want to be the rodeo queen."

Nothing like being put on the spot. What was her answer? Because Chad told me not to enter? She forced back a laugh. "Well, I think it's an honor to represent one's community in any way one can. The rodeo queen competition is a tradition here in Bakersville, and tradition means a lot to me."

"Why is that?" Dallas asked.

I don't know!

"Because...tradition is the backbone of any community. It's well-documented throughout history that human society cannot function in the absence of tradition."

"Miss Bay, one might call that an antiquated view," Dallas

said. "These days, some people claim that reason, rather than tradition, should guide humankind."

What? Catie hoped she had clenched her jaw before it dropped open. What the heck was he talking about? This didn't have anything to do with horses. Dallas McCray was trained as a lawyer, but didn't, to her knowledge, practice. Where was this philosophical stuff coming from? And what the heck was she supposed to say to that?

"Just who are these people who claim that, Mr. McCray?"

"Scientists, philosophers."

"I suppose one could argue the point," Catie said, "but we no longer live in a primitive society that depends solely on tradition. Traditions are no longer rigid and unbending. These days, reason and experience are certainly appropriate learning tools, but we shouldn't lose focus on tradition, either. The only way to continue to learn who we are, Mr. McCray, and where we're going, is to understand where we've been."

Dallas smiled, nodding, as he made notations on his pad of paper. "Very well said, Catie."

Now she was Catie again?

Okay, that was strange. She let out the breath she hadn't realized she was holding and forced herself to unclench her fists.

"I have a question," Chad said.

"Yes?"

"Catie, clearly you've indicated that the traditions of your hometown mean a lot to you."

"Yes, they certainly do."

"If that is the case," Chad said, "why did you leave your home for four years and not visit even one time?"

This time her mouth did drop open. She couldn't stop it.

"I think that's a question of a...a personal nature."

"Not at all," Chad said. "You've indicated your love of tradition."

"I can love my hometown and its traditions and still leave. The two aren't mutually exclusive."

"She's right, Chad," Zach said.

"I'm not sure I agree, Zach," Chad said. "She left for four years, and now she's not even back for a week before she plunges head first into the rodeo queen contest. And as far as I could tell, you never had any interest in this type of tradition before you left, Catie."

"Chad." Zach again.

"It's all right, Zach," Catie said, hoping she could speak without stammering, "I will answer Chad's question." She forced her eyes to his.

"I left because I was tired of Bakersville. I've lived here since I was a toddler, as you all well know. Unlike my older brother and sister, I don't know any other home. I wanted to get beyond the small-town life. Beyond the trips to Denver and the western slope. The chance came to attend the Sorbonne, and I jumped at it. Instead of coming home for vacations, I chose to travel. I've been all over Europe and some of Asia. I've seen riches and poverty, happiness and sadness. I've seen cultures that are millennia older than our own. And I loved every minute of it.

"But when I got off that plane a week ago and got back to Bakersville, it hit me that this was home. I had taken it for granted. I'm not proud of that, but I did. Not that I'd trade my four years overseas. They were wonderful, and I'll treasure them always. But Bakersville is home, and its traditions are important to me."

She said the words with emotion and conviction, and to her surprise, she found that she meant every single one.

"This pageant is a tradition, and should I emerge the winner, I will be proud to represent this community and its traditions to the best of my ability."

Dallas smiled. "I'm not sure that could have been said any better, Catie."

"I agree," Zach said.

Chad simply scowled.

"I don't have any more questions," Dallas said. "Do either of you?"

"Nope," Zach said.

"Chad?"

He cleared his throat. "No, nothing."

"But don't you want to ask me about horses?" Catie said. "Or the rodeo?"

Dallas chuckled. "We've known you since you could hardly talk, Catie-bug. We know you know more about horses than any of those other girls. You did fine. Now get on out of here."

Catie breathed a sigh of eternal relief, stood, and left the room.

★ ★ ★

"What in the name of God was that all about?" Dallas glowered at Chad.

"Yeah, I'd like to know, too," Zach said. "You grilled that poor girl to within an inch of her life on something that has no bearing on whether she'll make a good rodeo queen."

"Me?" Chad scoffed. "Dallas's the one who insisted on the

philosophy lesson."

"Hey, I just wanted to see what they taught her at that fancy French university. I have to say, I'm impressed."

"She was always a smart cookie, Dallas," Zach said.

"Yeah, you're right," Dallas agreed. "Annie thinks the world of her."

"I'd still like to know what you had up your ass," Zach said to Chad. "You went way overboard."

"It was a fair question," Chad said. "None of those others went gallivanting around for four years."

"True," Zach said, "but they didn't all grow up here either. A few of them just moved here, your girlfriend Amber, for instance."

"She's not my girlfriend."

"You took her to the Bay party."

"So? I brought Marnie, too. I'm sure as hell not dating my dog!"

"Always joking, aren't you?" Dallas said. "When in hell are you going to get serious about someone?"

"Oh, hmmm." Chad scratched his head, falsely contemplating. "I'd say around...the fifth of never."

Dallas shook his head. "You don't know what you're missing, boy."

"Boy?"

"Yeah, boy. You're just an overgrown kid with a teenage libido. Having a woman you love to come home to is damn nice. Damn comforting. Ain't it, Zach?"

"The man speaks the truth, Chad."

"Shit, Zach. I expect this kind of big brother bullshit from Dallas, but you? We used to be pals."

"We're still pals. I'm just concerned."

"Dallas didn't marry Annie till he was thirty-six."

"But Dallas was married to someone else before Annie."

"A big mistake, too," Dallas said, "but worth it. I wouldn't know Annie otherwise."

"I think I might be sick all over my score sheets," Chad said. "Do we have any more of these damn interviews? If there's a God in heaven, Catie was the last one."

Zach laughed. "Sit yourself down and hold back your puke. We've got two more ladies to see."

"Christ," Chad muttered, and picked up his pen. "Bring the next one in then."

CHAPTER ELEVEN

Sweat beaded on Catie's brow. The summer evening was hot, and her nerves were shot. What really irked her was that now she wanted to win this stupid competition. She was proud to be part of this community, proud it was her home. Who'd have thought?

She stood, dressed in a denim prairie skirt and a fluffy white peasant blouse—Annie's idea. *Why not look a little different?* she'd said—next to Amber, in line with the other thirteen contestants in the rodeo arena.

Amber wore a slim-fitting leather western style skirt and a sapphire silk western shirt. Her ostrich boots matched the shade of her shirt. Patti and all the others wore similar styles, very slimming and western. Catie felt a little like a frump. Why had she trusted Annie? The peasant look worked with Annie's Italian gypsy looks, but Catie had a sleeker beauty, a more western look. Heck, she'd grown up on a ranch. She should be looking the part. And she had the height. A straight skirt looked great on her. What in God's name had she been thinking?

"It's been a great competition," the emcee said into his microphone. "Our judges, the McCray boys, said it was a tough call. But we do have our winner and our first runner-up. May I have a drum roll, please?"

The drum roll came from a keyboard, but what the heck.

"Our first runner-up is...Miss Amber Cross!"

Amber jumped up, gave Catie a quick hug, and walked forward to receive her bouquet of roses.

Catie's heart slumped. If the judges—the McCrays—liked Amber, they wouldn't like her. She and Amber were different as night and day.

"Now, Amber, being first runner-up is very important. If, for any reason, our winner can't fulfill her duties as Bakersville's rodeo queen, you will step in for the remainder of the year."

"I'm honored, really," Amber said into the mike. "Thank you all!"

"Now for our winner. There's only one woman here who can outshine Amber. Do you have an idea who she is?"

"Catie!" Someone called from the stands.

Catie's cheeks warmed. Someone was making fun of her. This was awful.

"You got that right," the emcee said. "This year's rodeo queen is...Miss Caitlyn Bay!"

Patti and another girl grabbed Catie in a bear hug. Once she had wrangled free, she headed to the stage to join Amber. The emcee thrust a huge bouquet of red and white roses at her and put a rhinestone tiara on her head.

"It's good to have you back in Bakersville, Catie," the emcee said. "Do you have anything to say to the audience?"

"Uh, yes, of course," Catie said. "I'd like to thank the judges, of course. Your confidence in me means so much. And all the other contestants were wonderful. It was fun meeting you all and hanging out for the week. Amber, I'm so glad we met."

Sheesh. What else could she say?

"I'm looking forward to representing my city during the

coming year."

Thunderous applause followed, and Catie stood, mesmerized. She'd always known the people of Bakersville took this competition seriously, but now that she was the object of their affection and applause, an arrow of warmth shot through her body. They were pleased to have her as their rodeo queen.

She wouldn't let them down.

"Well said, Catie," the emcee continued. "As you know, tonight you'll reign over the rodeo competition. We have a special treat tonight. Zach and Dusty McCray have brought their bull, El Diablo, out, and are still offering that half-mil purse to anyone who can ride him for a full eight seconds. We'll have some barrel racing and bronc busting, some calf roping and trick riding, and all kinds of other good stuff. Get your hot dogs and funnel cakes from Mary at the concession stand. Now, Catie, if you'll join me in the announcer's box, we'll get this rodeo started!"

Catie followed the emcee—his name was Mark and he was new in town—to the box and watched the rodeo. Zach McCray won the bull-riding competition, staying on Stormtrooper for his eight seconds and garnering a nine point one from the judges. Chad didn't ride, which disappointed Catie. He was a good bull-rider, and she hadn't seen him ride for over four years.

When the rodeo competition was over, Catie went with Harper to the Bullfrog. She felt conspicuous in her tiara, but the throngs of people welcomed her. She danced with one cowboy after another, including Mark, the emcee, who had taken a particular liking to her.

Zach and Dallas weren't there. Not surprising. They were

family men with small children at home. But where was Chad?

As if in answer to her query, she spied him in a dark corner of the bar, in a clench with Amber. Were they kissing? Catie couldn't tell.

What nerve! She yearned to march right up to him and put a stop to this obscene public display.

But what could she do? Chad wasn't hers. He'd made that perfectly clear.

Or had he? She was the one who'd walked out of his hotel room Wednesday night when he'd wanted to make love. Of course, he had eventually agreed with her and had apologized for putting her in a difficult position.

Anger seethed in Catie's gut. Ethics or none, she was no more than a lay to him. A novelty he'd obviously gotten over. He thought she was too young. So why wasn't Amber too young? Catie had found out from the other girl that she was twenty-one as well.

Yeah, Catie was angry. But all the anger in the world wouldn't erase the love she had for that stupid cowboy.

Chad McCray was the love of her life, and he always would be.

★ ★ ★

"I'm sorry, honey. I just don't think we were meant to be together."

Amber tightened her hold on Chad. "I don't understand. A week ago you couldn't wait to get me in the sack, and now you put me off and put me off."

"You're young, for one thing."

"I'm nearly twenty-two. You'll have to come up with a

better excuse. Is there someone else?"

"Hell, no."

"Then what on earth is going on?"

"I'm just not into...relationships is all."

"A few dates does not a relationship make, Chad. I guess we really don't know each other that well. I could have sworn you were a guy who liked to have fun."

"Well, sure I do."

"Then there's someone else. It's Catie, isn't it?"

"For God's sake, there's no one else, Amber. I just don't want to get involved with anyone right now." He physically removed her arms from around his waist. "You're a real nice girl. Beautiful and sweet. You earned that runner-up position, and it was no easy task, you being new in town and all."

"Did you vote for me, Chad?" Amber asked. "Or did you vote for Caitlyn?"

"There were three judges, Amber."

"But who was your choice?"

"I can't say. It's not fair of you to ask me."

"Your choice was Caitlyn, then."

"I didn't say that."

"You didn't have to." Amber stood on her tiptoes and brushed her lips lightly against Chad's cheek. "I think we'd have fun together, cowboy, but I guess it's not to be. It was nice meeting you."

She walked away, into the crowd of people celebrating.

Damn. Chad gritted his teeth. What the hell was wrong with him? He could have had her six different ways by now, but he just wasn't interested.

He glanced across the room. Catie stood talking to Harper, her tiara twinkling.

But it was no match for her eyes or her smile.

He stroke toward her with purpose.

"Hey, rodeo queen," he drawled, "wanna dance?"

He grinned as a telltale blush colored her pretty face.

"You don't mind, do you, Harper?" Chad asked.

"No. Of course not."

"Then, come on, Catie. Let's cut the rug."

"Wait one minute," she said. "Why would you just assume I'm going to dance with you? Why don't you dance with Harper? He said he didn't mind."

"Catie—" Harper said.

"A gentleman would wait for my answer," Catie continued.

"Sugar, if you don't know by now, let me fill you in." He grabbed her arm and dragged her to the crowded dance floor. "I ain't no gentleman."

He pulled her against his body and reveled in her warmth, her softness. Why couldn't he get enough of her? She was so young, so innocent.

Well, not so innocent anymore. He'd taken care of that. He was probably the first in a long line of lovers she'd have. A knife sliced into his gut. Why should that bother him? He didn't want her. Well, not true. He wanted her. Just not forever. And she deserved forever.

Forever with a man who loved her.

So why was the thought of any man touching her so horrible? So vile? He squeezed her close, and her small gasp rang in his ears.

"Let's go," he said, pulling her off the dance floor and toward the door of the Bullfrog.

"Chad? What's going on?"

He pulled her out the door and around to the parking

lot behind the bar. Several couples laughed intimately in the shadows. Chad headed for his pickup and pushed her against the driver's side. He clamped his mouth down on hers.

"Mmmpphhhh." Her voice was muffled against his seeking tongue.

He forced her lips open and plunged inside. Sweet God, lime and raspberries again. Did this woman know how to bewitch him? He'd never tasted anything so intoxicating.

He ripped his mouth from hers. "What have you done to me, sugar?"

"I... I haven't done anything, Chad."

"You've bespelled me. Bewitched me."

"You're being silly. Don't joke like that."

Her voice was sweeter than the softest tune on a flute. He pressed his lips to her neck, raining kisses on her smooth skin and inhaling her fresh outdoorsy scent. "I want you, Catie. I want you in my bed."

"Oh, Chad." Her exhale was a whispered caress against his neck.

"Let's go."

"I... I can't."

"Why not?" He nibbled her ear. "The competition's over. You won. No more ethical problems."

"Because. I don't want a roll in the hay."

"I know, sugar. I know."

"Chad." She pushed at his chest.

He held her firmly. "What?"

"Why did you pick me?"

"Because you were the prettiest, had the most poise, and no one can beat you on horseback."

"But was I *your* choice?"

"Yeah. You were. But my vote on the fashion show got disqualified."

"Disqualified? Why?"

He beamed. "Because I gave you a twelve."

"So?"

"The highest score I could give was ten. But baby, a ten for you in that hot green bikini wasn't near high enough."

The cute redness on her cheeks glowed, even in the moonlight.

"It's a gorgeous night," he said. "You wanna go riding again?"

"I... It's not a good idea, Chad."

"Sugar, it's a fucking great idea." He nipped the softness of her neck. "You ever fantasize about making love on horseback?" he whispered.

"I told you—"

"Right, no roll in the hay." He chuckled. "We'll go back to my place. No hay there. I promise." He licked her pulse point and enjoyed the sweet shudder that flowed through her. Her body responded to him like no other woman's had.

"Yeah. Yeah. Okay. A ride."

"Come on." He opened the door of his truck, walked her around to the passenger side, and helped her in. "Let's go."

★ ★ ★

They never made it on the moonlight ride. Chad took Catie back to his place and they ended up in bed.

Catie didn't fight it. He was right. The ethics were moot at this point, and here was another chance to make love with the man she adored.

She took it, even knowing it would lead to more heartache.

They explored each other's bodies with new enthusiasm.

Catie took Chad's cock into her mouth, and the sensation of his sleek hardness, the salty and masculine taste, the groans of satisfaction from low in his throat—all added up to delicious and amazing. She licked around the base, explored his sac, buried her nose in his black curls and inhaled. She licked the shaft, curling her tongue around his head and then thrusting her entire mouth upon him. Up and down, up and down. His hips lifted in tandem with her strokes, and he moaned her name, his husky voice music to her ears.

"Ah, Catie. Sugar."

She looked upward, her eyes meeting his. They smoked. His half-lidded dark eyes actually smoked.

"Come here," he said.

She let his cock drop from her mouth and kissed the head. He shivered.

"Damn, Catie, if you don't come here, this is going to be over in another second."

She climbed forward.

"Drawer," he said. "Condom."

She reached into the drawer of his night table and grabbed a condom. When she handed it to him, he shook his head, a sly smile curving on his lips.

"You do it."

"Me?" She had never put a condom on a man before. Well, of course she hadn't. She'd been a virgin.

"Yeah, you. It's something...special between a man and a woman. I want you to do it."

"But I don't know what I'm doing."

"Shh. Baby, you'll do fine. Just take it out, pinch the tip of the rubber to leave a little space for the...you know. Then put it on me."

"Are you sure you want me to?"

"God, sugar. Yeah, I want you to."

Catie inhaled sharply and ripped the foil packet open. The condom was light beige, made out of lambskin, the package said. It had a little lubricant on it, and it was so thin and fragile she wasn't sure it could protect against anything. The image of the torn condom from earlier slid into her mind, and she quickly banished it. There was no reason to worry. She pinched the tip, as Chad had told her, and slowly rolled it onto his huge cock.

"Yeah, sugar, just like that," he said. "Just like that. Come here." He pulled her toward him. "Ride me, baby. Ride me into the sunrise."

Catie sank down onto him, letting him fill her so completely, so thoroughly. It felt different this way, from a different angle. It felt so damn good.

"God, sugar. That's nice."

"Yeah. Yeah it is." Catie crossed her arms. She felt so exposed, sitting on top of Chad. Everything was in full view.

"Don't cover yourself, baby. You're so beautiful. Such gorgeous breasts." He leaned forward and clasped his lips around one nipple. "Mmmm. Delicious. Sugar nipples."

Catie's breath caught, and she continued to move up and down on Chad, until she felt the still new contractions begin deep within her body.

"Oh, Chad!" she cried.

Chad let her nipple slide from his mouth. "That's it, sugar. Come. Come for me. Come all over me." He thrust upward, into her, filling her. "Ah, yeah. That's it."

Catie collapsed on Chad's chest, his mat of hair slick with perspiration. Her ear slid over his heart, and its beat thumped against her, quick, in synchrony with hers.

Oh, how I love this man.

"Stay with me, sugar."

"Hmmm?"

"Stay. Spend the night with me. Please."

Warmth radiated through her. "Really?"

"I don't ask a lot of women to stay, Catie. I can't promise you anything beyond tomorrow, but I want you to be here in the morning."

Catie's lips curved against Chad's hard chest, and she nodded.

"Okay, Chad. I'll stay."

CHAPTER TWELVE

Catie woke up in Chad's arms. A dream come true.

"Hey, sugar." He nuzzled her neck.

"The parade, Chad. I have to ride in the parade."

"Mmm. Later, baby." He trailed moist, sucking kisses over her neck, her chest, her nipples. "You're so sweet."

"But I need to shower, and get my outfit. It's at home."

Chad chuckled, a rumble against the sensitive skin of Catie's breasts. "You already had an outfit? Just assumed you'd win?"

"Angie's idea."

She shuddered. His mouth was so firm, so demanding, and it felt so good on her flesh.

"I'm not surprised." He sucked a nipple between his lips.

Catie closed her eyes, her head flinging backward.

"Delicious," Chad said against her skin.

"The parade—"

"Fuck the parade," he rasped against her skin. "Better yet, I'm going to fuck you."

He reached between her legs and slid his long fingers through her folds. "Mmm. Always wet, sugar. Always wet for me."

Of course she was. Her body was in a perpetual state of heat around him. This couldn't be normal, could it? Even his crude words turned her on.

"Chad."

"Yeah, baby, say my name. I love that."

"I wasn't—"

"Say it again. I love the way it rolls off your tongue."

"Chad."

"Yeah, just like that."

He slid one long finger inside her, and she sighed. Her whole body blazed. So good.

"I'm going to make you come, sugar." He slid down her body, leaving wet kisses as he went.

She shivered and quaked beneath his talented hands and mouth.

"I'm going to make you come so hard that you cream all over my face, and then I'm going to stuff my hard cock inside you so deep, bury myself in that sweetness."

Catie gasped as his mouth descended to her most private place.

To hell with the parade.

★ ★ ★

No big surprise. Catie was late to the parade. But only by a few minutes. She wouldn't let Chad drive her either. She felt it wouldn't make the right statement for her to be seen with one of the judges the day after the competition had ended.

Chad had agreed, though a little too quickly for Catie's taste. She knew he wasn't serious about her. Heck, had he ever been serious about any woman? Nope. And she wasn't about to be the first. Rationally, she knew this. But a little part of her hoped she'd be the one to land the unattainable Chad McCray.

But they weren't in love. At least he wasn't.

They weren't even dating. They were sleeping together.

On his schedule. When *he* wanted it. And she wanted him so much she was willing to go along.

Was she completely blind?

No, she knew who and what he was. Still, she loved him.

"Come on, Catie," Judy Williamson called, "we need you and Ladybird over here. You'll be leading the parade."

Ladybird was curried and saddled and ready to go, so Catie led her in the direction from which Judy's voice had come. The Bakersville High School marching band was lining up, the band director yelling. The pom-pom girls were giggling and pointing at cute boys.

Catie rolled her eyes. She'd never been a pom-pom. Nope, never one for that high school stuff. Of course with her clumsiness, she'd have fallen off the pyramid anyway. She'd been content to be the bookworm, the A student, the girl who preferred the company of horses to two-legged creatures.

Unless the two-legged creature's name was Chad McCray.

God, was she back to him again? Would her thoughts ever be free of him?

She shook her head and sighed. Not as long as she kept sleeping with him, they wouldn't. She knew something else as well.

She'd continue sleeping with him. For as long as he'd have her.

She mounted Ladybird and took her place at the head of the parade with the grand marshal, who happened to be Dallas McCray.

"Hey there, rodeo queen," Dallas said, his dark eyes crinkling at the corners. He was handsome, no doubt. He and Zach resembled each other. They looked like their mother,

Laurie, who'd had the jet-black hair. Chad looked more like their late father, Jason McCray, whose hair had been dark, but a shade or two shy of black. Jason's had never grayed. Even when he'd passed on ten years ago at the age of seventy, his hair was still that warm dark brown, like Chad's. Dallas had been graying for years, and now Zach had started. It worked on them. But not Chad. Course he was younger, but Catie secretly hoped he'd remain gray-free forever. She loved the walnut warmth of his hair color. The way it felt when she ran her fingers through its silkiness. How it whispered against her thighs when his head was between her legs.

Did she really taste like raspberries?

"You gonna answer me?"

She jerked in the saddle. "What?"

Dallas chuckled. "You were a million miles away, rodeo queen."

Her cheeks warmed. Good thing he couldn't read her mind. She was having some very lascivious thoughts about his baby brother. "I'm sorry, Dallas. What did you ask?"

"I asked whether you had any big plans after the parade. Annie and I are having some people over. We just threw it together this morning."

"Oh. I...uh..." Chad hadn't said anything about getting together with her. Likely he'd be at his brother's house. "No, no, I don't have any plans."

"Then stop by. Annie'd love for you to be there."

"Sure, I'd love to."

"Great. Just come by after the parade. It's a pretty casual affair. Annie ordered up barbecue from Dixon's this morning."

"Mmm. Sounds yummy."

"You seen Chad this morning?"

Catie's pulse jumpstarted, and she hoped the warmth that she knew reddened her looked like nothing more than summer heat. She cleared her throat. "No, I haven't."

"Okay. I need to tell him about our shindig." He tipped his Stetson and trotted off on his gray gelding. "See you later. I'm off. Judy'll tell you when to go."

"Okay. Thanks, Dallas."

Behind her, the band was tuning up. Among the discord and din of voices, Catie heard Amber trot up next to her.

"Hey there," the other woman said.

"Amber. Hi!" Catie was genuinely glad to see her. "Are you in the parade, too?"

"Yeah, they asked me. I'm supposed to ride up here with you."

"That's great. I've been gone for a while, but I'm glad they're letting the first runner-up ride. That's awesome."

"Didn't they do it before?"

"Honestly, I never paid much attention. The last parade I attended was five years ago." She laughed. "I always paid more attention the horses than the people riding them."

Amber laughed, and her smile seemed genuine. Maybe they would be friends.

Judy motioned for them to go, and Catie and Amber trotted along behind a few floats. Amber was incredibly good at this. She waved and smiled and didn't look out of place at all in her first runner-up sash. Catie felt like a fish out of water. Amber definitely should have won the contest. She might not be the horsewoman Catie was, but she had the poise thing down. Catie was glad she didn't have to walk in the parade. She'd likely trip over someone's banana peel or something.

★ ★ ★

Chad didn't like it. He didn't like it one bit. That skunk Joe Bradley was hanging all over Catie. Why was he at Dallas's anyway?

Annie. That's right. He and Annie were friends. He'd taken her out on a date when she and Dallas were broken up. Or before they got together. Or whatever. Chad never could keep it straight. His brother had been an idiot. He'd let Annie go.

Course who was Chad to talk? Was he just as much of an idiot when it came to Catie?

He sure didn't want anything serious. Or so he thought.

Still, he responded to her in a way different from any woman he'd known. What was it about her? She was beautiful, but Chad had known lots of beautiful women.

She was so damn young, though. Why in hell couldn't he keep his hands to himself around her?

She was flirting with Joe, damn her. As if he, Chad, weren't even here. It was his brother's house, for God's sake. Of course he was here, and Catie should be with him.

But he'd leave her be. She was the rodeo queen. Everyone wanted to talk to her, congratulate her. That's probably all it was. That's why Joe was hanging around her. He and all those other young men.

Hell, Joe was four years older than Chad!

Enough was enough.

His long strides carried him straight toward Catie and her male harem.

"Hey, Chad," Joe said. "Come to join the party?"

"Come to take away the queen," Chad said. "C'mon,

Catie."

"What?" Catie looked at him suspiciously. "Terry was in the middle of a story, Chad. Why don't you join us?"

"I don't think so." He grabbed her arm. "We need to chat."

"We do?"

"Yeah. Excuse us, will you fellas?"

"Uh, sure," Joe said, nodding to the others. "But don't keep her away too long."

"What is this all about?" Catie demanded, as Chad pulled her into the house and down a long hallway to Dallas's office. He shut the door and turned the deadbolt.

"Joe's not your type."

"What?"

"You heard me."

"I don't have a type, Chad. And it doesn't matter anyway. I'm not interested in Joe."

"He's sure interested in you."

"He's old enough to be my daddy, Chad!"

"He's only four years older than I am, sugar."

"Okay, my young daddy. Jesus."

"He wasn't lookin' at you like a daddy looks at his little girl."

"This is stupid." Catie shrugged loose from his grasp. "I want to get back to the party."

"You like being queen for day, huh?"

"Queen for the year, Chad McCray. I'm queen for a year. And hell yeah, I'm beginning to like it. I've never gotten this much attention from..."

Her cheeks pinked. Damn, she was adorable as all get out.

"From men, sugar? You've never had this much attention from men?"

"No," she said flatly. "No, I have not. And frankly, Chad, it's flattering and I like it. So if you'll excuse me—"

He clamped his mouth on hers so hard he thought for sure he'd bruised his lips. She resisted at first, but his persistence paid off, and she sighed and opened to him. He swept his tongue into her mouth, tasting her lips, her teeth, the inside of her cheeks. He hadn't a clue what she'd been drinking, but damn it, she tasted like raspberries. Again. He groaned. Why couldn't he get enough of her?

As though it had a mind of its own, one of his hands began to unsnap her white western shirt. The shirt was fitted—the same one she'd worn in the parade, and it clung to the swell of her finely shaped breasts and had made him hard all freaking day.

She shied away.

"Nuh-uh, sugar," he whispered. "You're not getting away from me."

She pushed against his chest, but he held her in his grasp.

"I want you." He ripped all the snaps open with one fell swoop.

"You just had me last night." Catie pushed against his chest.

"Well, I want you again now."

"No, Chad. Not like this. Not in your brother's house, with the whole town outside."

Chad chuckled, nipping her ear. "I remember a party once. At your house. And you would have been damn happy to do this with the whole damn town within earshot."

Chad's arousal tightened even more, if that were possible, as he thought of the gazebo on the Bay ranch, and that night four years earlier when Catie had begged him to make love to her. He had resisted, but he still dreamed of that night. Even though he'd had her several times now, the memories of that evening still inflamed his passions. Would he always be inflamed around Catie Bay?

Catie pushed him away, and her strength startled him.

"I was a kid then, Chad, as you reminded me that night. I no longer want to make love in front of the whole damn town."

"Fine then." He took her hand. "We'll go back to my place."

"No again," she said.

Chad gasped in surprise. "What?"

"You heard me."

He shook his head. "Unbelievable."

"What's so unbelievable about it? We had some good times. You made it clear that's all I could ever expect from you. I enjoyed myself. You did your...job well."

"My job? What the fuck?"

"Yeah. Your job of taking my virginity."

"Now you hold on, sugar. That's not fair."

"It's not? Well, here's some news, Chad McCray. I got what I wanted. I got you to take my virginity. I wanted it. I got it. I'm done."

Chad shook his head, flabbergasted. Was he hearing her right? "You're kidding."

"Nope." Catie shook her head with vehemence. "I want you. I don't deny it. But I'm no longer satisfied to come to your bed just when you're in the mood. You have a decision to make, Chad. I'm not going to be your call girl any longer."

"Call girl?" Did she really think he thought of her that way? "I've never paid for sex in my life, and I ain't gonna start now, sugar."

"Good. You don't have to. There's a whole ranch full of beautiful women out back, Chad. One of them's bound to strike your fancy. And I'm sure she'll offer it up for free. But this little filly's done."

She snapped up her shirt, fluffed her hair, walked toward the door, and turned the deadbolt.

"Catie," he said, but she was already gone.

★ ★ ★

Catie stood in the powder room, splashing cold water over her face.

She had done the right thing. Chad wasn't serious about her, and she couldn't keep sleeping with him. Oh, she wanted to, and only a day ago, she had been determined to keep it up. But talking to the other men had made her realize that maybe, just maybe, there was a man out there who would care for her. Would offer her more than just sex when he was horny.

She was worth more, damn it. And she intended to have it.

A tear trickled down her cheek.

Too bad she only wanted it from one man, and he was the one who would never give it to her.

CHAPTER THIRTEEN

Two weeks had passed, and he hadn't called.

Not that Catie was surprised. Chad hadn't promised anything beyond the next day, and waking up in his arms and making love again had been totally worth it.

Now, Catie was driving into Murphy. She had an errand to run, and she couldn't do it in Bakersville. Couldn't risk the small-town gossip.

She needed a home pregnancy test.

Her fears had surfaced. She was three days late.

She walked through the pharmacy in the small cow town, feeling conspicuous. They all knew why she was here, didn't they? Their stares melded to her flesh. Their judgments mocked her. She took a deep breath and walked down one aisle and then another, mindlessly throwing items in her basket. A candy bar. Cotton balls. A knock-off of Chanel No. 5. She felt like a teenage boy buying condoms. This was ridiculous.

Condoms. That's probably where she'd find the pregnancy tests. Ha. Ironic. She came upon the birth control aisle and perused the packages. *Ribbed for her pleasure.* Yeah, whatever.

Sure enough, the home pregnancy tests sat on a shelf next to the ovulation predictors. She grabbed one of the boxes that had two tests. Might as well be sure, right?

On her way out, she threw a trashy novel into her basket. There, she had several things other than the pregnancy test. This looked perfectly normal, right? She was probably a married woman buying some bath items and a book, and oh, yeah, by the way, a pregnancy test.

Her ringless left hand seemed to glow.

The teenage clerk rang up her purchases without a sideways glance. *Breathe in, breathe out.* Catie was convinced she'd hyperventilate at any moment.

She ran to her car and sat down, inhaling.

She needed to do the pregnancy test now. She couldn't wait until she got home. She stuck the box in her purse and walked into the grocery store next to the pharmacy. She headed straight to the back where the restrooms usually were.

She eased into a stall and sat on the toilet. She opened the box and read through the instructions quickly. So this was what she had been reduced to. Peeing on a stick in a public restroom.

Here goes nothing.

After following the instructions, she hid the stick in the test box and watched the second hand on her watch.

Had three minutes always been this slow?

Ticktock, ticktock, ticktock.

Insanity threatened to overtake her.

When the second hand finally hit the twelve, nausea rose in her gut, and her skin tightened.

She slowly withdrew the stick from the box.

★ ★ ★

Chad missed Catie.

He finally admitted it to himself. He was going to ask her on a real date. Dinner, maybe a movie, and then sex back at his place.

He chuckled. His brothers would give him three shades of shit for this.

Damn, she was so young. But he'd been ready to hit the hay with Amber, and she was nearly as young as Catie. Funny thing was, he didn't think of Amber that way. He didn't remember Amber as a cute little toddler.

He thought of his brother Zach, who had married Dusty O'Donovan, seven years his junior. Dusty had been the daughter of one of the McCrays' ranch hands. They left the ranch when Dusty was six and Zach was thirteen, and the two met up again seventeen years later.

But Zach hadn't watched Dusty grow into an awkward prepubescent, a pretty freckle-faced teen, and a drop-dead gorgeous woman. Would it have been different for Zach if he had?

Plus, Catie and Chad were eleven years apart, four more than Zach and Dusty. Hell, what did it matter?

She was a woman and he was attracted to her. Attracted as he'd never been before.

He picked up his cell phone and called the Bay house. Why had he never thought to get Catie's cell number?

"Hello."

"Hi, Maria. It's Chad McCray."

"Chad, how are you? Are you calling for Wayne?"

"No, ma'am."

"Harper then?"

"Uh, no. I'd like to speak to Catie, please."

"Oh. Goodness."

Clearly, Catie hadn't told her mother where she'd spent the night a few weeks ago.

"Is she there?"

"She ran a few errands. Can I have her call you later?"

"Uh..." He wanted to call *her*. Not have her return his call. He wanted to do this right.

What? Who was that voice inside his head, and what had it done with Chad McCray?

"No, ma'am. Thank you. I'll call back later."

"Okay, Chad. Bye now."

Damn, if only he had her cell number.

He felt like a schoolboy rather than a thirty-two-year-old man, giddy over a first date with a girl he really liked. A girl he wanted more than anything. A girl who could steal his heart.

His heart? Since when had his heart become involved? He'd liked women before, had feelings for them, but never had he felt this yearning for closeness. Not just the closeness of bodies either.

He jolted from his thoughts when his cell phone rang. He looked down. He didn't recognize the number.

"Yeah?"

"Chad?"

Catie's voice. Damn, had her mother told her to call him? "Hi there, sugar. I was just thinking about you."

"Oh." Then, "You were?"

Something was off in her voice. She sounded sad, remorseful. "Did your ma tell you I called?"

"Uh, no, she didn't. I'm not home. I'm in my car."

"Yeah, she said you were running errands. You close by?"

"Not too far," she said. "I...uh...need to talk to you."

"I want to talk to you, too, sugar. You want to come over?"

"We need to talk in private, Chad."

"Nothing more private than my bedroom, baby."

Silence. What was wrong? He wanted her to come over

so he could take her in his arms and promise her everything would be okay. That he'd make it okay for her.

Who was this stranger?

"I... I can't come over for that, Chad."

"Okay."

Don't push. You want to take her on a real date, remember? The sex'll come later.

"Let's meet somewhere private."

"Just come over here, Catie. I promise I'll keep my hands to myself. I'll have Brenda whip us up some sandwiches for lunch, okay? You hungry?"

"No. Not particularly."

"What's wrong, sugar?"

"Nothing I can talk about now. I'll tell you when I get there, okay?"

"Okay, baby." He smiled into the phone. "I'll be waiting."

★ ★ ★

Positive.

The dang thing was positive.

Catie drove onto the McCray property and edged her way to Chad's ranch house. How could she tell him? He had taken precautions. Maybe she should have gone on birth control pills a while back as an extra back-up. But she hadn't been sexually active, so what would have been the point? Or she should have carried some spermicidal suppositories in her purse. Even if she had, would she have bothered with them when Chad put on a condom?

She shook her head. No more second guessing. What was done was done, and she and Chad had to figure out what to do about it together.

She hadn't trapped him. The condom breaking had been an unfortunate accident. Nothing more. He would understand that.

Should she have told him about the condom? She hadn't wanted to worry him unnecessarily over an eleven percent possibility.

Again, it didn't really matter. Chad knew he had used a condom. He couldn't accuse her of trapping him. She would never have done that to him anyway. She loved him too much.

If she was going to have him, she wanted all of him. His love. His devotion. His whole heart and soul.

What would he do?

More importantly, what would he want *her* to do?

Because she had made up her mind about one thing already. Whether he decided to be involved or not, she was having this baby.

CHAPTER FOURTEEN

"Hey there, rodeo queen," Chad drawled when he opened the door for Catie.

He looked gorgeous, as usual. His snug fitting jeans hugged his firm rear-end and sat below his hips at just the right angle to show off the cuts in his hip bones. He wasn't wearing a shirt, damn him. His golden muscular chest made her heart race.

He reached toward her. "You been crying, sugar?"

Crying. Bawling. Heck, yes. He'd be crying in a minute, too. She sniffed. "A little."

"What on earth is wrong? Can I help?"

"I don't know that you can, Chad." Catie stifled a sob. "But I do need to talk to you."

"Well, now, come on in, then." He led her to the kitchen. "Brenda whipped us up a nice lunch. You want some tea?" He grinned. "Some raspberry tea?"

Catie's tummy lurched at the thought of food. It was too early for morning sickness. She had a couple of more weeks before that lovely part of pregnancy set in. Nope, this nausea came from having to tell perpetual bachelor Chad McCray that he was about to become a father.

"Tea'd be fine, but I can't eat. I'm not feeling quite myself."

"All right. Sit on down." He motioned to his kitchen table. "I'll get you some tea, and then you can tell me what's got that pretty face all in a frown."

He brought her tea, sat down next to her, took her hand, and rubbed his thumb into her palm. It felt warm. It felt good.

"Catie, there's something I need to say to you."

"What?"

"Well, I hope this'll help you feel better. Course I might be overestimating my importance in your life." He looked into his lap. "But I sure hope not. Anyway"—he took her other hand—"I'd like to...*see* you. Romantically. You know, take you on a date. Get to know each other better."

Her heart sank. Was her dream actually coming true? Now that she had to tell him she was pregnant? Tears threatened behind her eyes. "Chad—"

"Let me finish." He cleared his throat. "I know we went to bed quickly. I wanted it. I don't have to tell you that."

"I wanted it too. And I meant it when I said you didn't owe me anything." *I still mean it*, Catie thought, *even though...* She couldn't finish the thought.

"I know you did, sugar. But I'm hoping you'll let me be more of a part of your life. I... I have strong feelings for you. I'd like to see where they could lead."

"Uh, well, sure, Chad. I'd like that, too, but—"

"But what, sugar?"

"I have something I have to tell you. I hope you'll be happy. I just don't know." She choked back another sob and sniffed.

Chad stood and brought a box of tissues to her.

"Thank you."

"No problem, sugar. I hate to see you like this. Is one of your horses sick?"

"No, no. Nothing like that."

"Then what is it? You can tell me. I'll help if I can."

How she hoped he'd help. How she hoped he wouldn't be

completely disappointed.

She took a deep breath. "Chad, I'm pregnant."

★ ★ ★

Chad inhaled, and his heart nearly skidded to a stop. *Pregnant. Baby.*

How many times could one man—one man who intended to remain single and childless—endure those words?

Within seconds, Chad relived the hellish two month nightmare he'd withstood the previous year—only a week after he'd buried his mother.

"Well, hi there," the pretty blond woman said when he opened his door on a warm summer evening. She held the hand of a little blond toddler.

"Can I help you, ma'am?" Chad asked.

"Don't you recognize me, Chad?"

"Uh...well. I'm sure sorry. Can't say that I do."

"Surely you remember that night we spent in Denver four years ago? During the stock show?" She winked. "I know I'll never forget it."

Stock show? Chad recognized her then. He'd met the woman at a party Angie and Harper had thrown. He and Dusty's brother, Sam, had taken off with this woman and her friend, barrel racer Sydney Buchanan. They'd gone to dinner, and then back to his hotel room...

"Yeah, yeah, Laura, right?"

"Linda." She continued to smile, but tension laced her lips.

"Linda, okay. What can I do for you?"

She let go of the little boy's hand and pushed him forward.

"I'd like you to meet your son."

★ ★ ★

Silence. His face had turned to granite. Had he gone completely devoid of emotion? Catie stood, pondering. Should she say something else?

Finally, "Good joke."

"It's not a joke."

"That's ridiculous. You can't be pregnant. We used protection."

"Yes. I know. But after that first night, I found one of your condoms by the trash in the morning. It... It had a tear in it."

"Impossible. I use the best there are. I've never had a problem before." He stood up and paced. "How can you be sure?"

"I'm a few days late. I drove into Murphy this morning and bought a home pregnancy test. It...was positive."

"Only a few days? Then that could be a mistake."

"Yeah. It could be, but it's not. This is the same thing they use at doctor's offices, Chad. They're so sensitive now that you can detect pregnancy before you even miss your period. I've already missed mine."

"Come on. You're going to a doctor. The best in Denver. We'll get to the bottom of this."

"Chad, I agree that I need to go to a doctor, but to start prenatal care, not to have a pregnancy test."

"Prenatal care? Oh my God."

"Chad, I—"

"A rip in the condom. Nearly twenty years of condom use, Catie, and I've never had one rip on me. Interesting, isn't it?"

"Wh-What do you mean?"

"What I mean is, that last time, you put the condom on me, remember?"

"So?"

"So it would have been really easy for you to poke a hole in it without me knowing."

Catie's blood boiled. "You are *not* going to pin this on me. I found the condom with the tear in it after the first time, before I ever put a condom on you. And for your information, I wished damn hard for that test to be negative. I knew you didn't want a child, a family. I knew you didn't want me. But it's positive, and the child is yours."

"Maybe."

She clenched her fists. "How *dare* you?"

"How do I know who you've been seeing? I've only been with you a few days out of the three weeks you've been home."

"You fucking bastard!" Catie stood and pushed her chair under the table loudly. "The baby is yours. The condom ripped. I had nothing to do with it."

"Get in my truck."

"I'm not going anywhere with you."

"The hell you're not. We're going to have a real doctor check you out. Then we'll figure out where we can go to get rid of this...problem."

"Get rid of it?" She gritted her teeth. "You can't be serious. Know one thing, Chad McCray. I'm having this baby. With or without you."

"Goddamnit."

"What's your problem anyway? A minute ago, you wanted to date me. To see me romantically, I believe is how you put it."

"Dating you and setting up house are two different

things."

"Setting up house? I haven't asked you for anything."

"The hell you haven't. Come on."

"No."

"Yes. We need to get you to a doctor in Denver. We need to find out what's going on."

"I already know what's going on. I'm having a baby. You're the father. I'm not asking you for anything. You can be involved or not. It's your choice, but I'm having this child."

Chad's muscles tightened visibly. "If you're bound and determined, you're coming with me. I want a real doctor to look at you, Catie."

He said not another word as he pulled her out of the kitchen, out of the house, and into his pickup.

He said not a word during the two-hour drive to Denver.

He said not a word as he pulled her into the OB-GYN department of Denver Memorial hospital and demanded to see the best doctor they had.

They waited another hour in the waiting area, and he said not a word.

When the doctor confirmed the pregnancy, pronounced Catie in excellent health, assured her she could still have intimate relations, and wrote her a prescription for prenatal vitamins, Chad finally spoke.

"Come on, then." He pulled her out of the doctor's office.

"Where are we going now?"

"To the courthouse. We're getting married."

CHAPTER FIFTEEN

In a pink haze, Catie became Mrs. Chad McCray.

No Papa giving her away. No Angie as her beautiful maid of honor. No white dress. No flowers. No Mama crying in the front row. No Mozart and no string quartet.

No passionate wedding kiss.

Just a quick signing of a marriage license and basic vows spoken in robotic tones.

She had married the man of her dreams.

In an event the opposite of what she had dreamed of for nearly her entire life.

He didn't want her. Except maybe sexually. Not enough. Not what she'd dreamed of.

He didn't love her.

But he felt responsible for her. For her and this child she was determined to bring into the world.

Had she been more herself, she might not have gone through with the wedding. But she had, and now she and Chad were driving back to Bakersville after dark.

"I... Where will I live?" The first words she'd spoken since "I do."

"At my place. You can have your own room."

"Oh." So that's how it would be. "I need to stop at my house, get some stuff."

"In the morning."

"But I need my... I need to tell my parents. About us.

About the baby."

"In the morning, Catie."

"Now. Please."

Chad pulled onto the side of the road and turned off the ignition. He turned to her, his eyes cold.

"Catie, this day has turned into something out of my nightmares. I will eventually have to tell your parents that I knocked up their baby girl. Out of wedlock."

"But it was an accident. We used protection. They'll understand."

Chad scoffed. "Your daddy'll understand? That I humped his daughter and got her with child? It sounds like a fucking lie, Catie, and I'm having a hard time believing it myself."

"But—"

"No buts. Tomorrow we'll deal with our families. Tonight I want to go home and go to bed." He turned on the ignition, looked straight ahead, and continued driving.

Catie's heart sank. Sadness welled within her. She wanted her mother. Her father. Her brother. Her own house. Her own bed. To be back in Paris. To be traveling. She longed to talk to Dominic, who had become her best friend. She wanted so much.

Most of all, she wanted Chad's love.

And here she found herself married to him. The man she loved, had always loved.

The father of her child.

How had things gone so horribly wrong?

When they finally arrived at Chad's house, he ushered her inside.

"The doctor said you can have sex."

"Well, yeah, but—"

"Then I, by God, want a wedding night. You'll stay with me tonight. You can move into one of the guest rooms tomorrow."

"No, Chad. I don't want to be...intimate with you tonight."

"I don't recall asking your opinion on the matter."

He grabbed her and kissed her. Hard. She gasped as his tongue plunged into her mouth. They had kissed before, but not like this. This was an angry kiss. A possessive kiss.

Despite herself, she enjoyed it. He held her so close she felt every inch of his muscle pressed against her. His masterful mouth devoured hers, and she felt, rather than heard, the moans from deep within his chest. She shivered as her passion grew. Though he was angry, she loved the warmth of his body pressed so close to hers. She tunneled her fingers through his silky hair, pulling him closer, and she caught his tongue between her lips and sucked it into her mouth, nursing on it like it contained the nectar of life. Like she couldn't get enough.

She couldn't.

He groaned again and ground his arousal into her belly. His body became more insistent. She bit his lip, his tongue, and then plunged her own into the firm drugging pressure of his mouth. The perfect kiss.

Without breaking the kiss, Chad lifted her and carried her to his bedroom.

★ ★ ★

He'd lost control.

Never had happened before, but he'd gone feral. This woman was carrying his child. He should show her the respect she deserved, but here he was acting like a caveman branding his woman.

Yet he couldn't stop.

He wanted her. Wanted to brand her. Wanted to possess her.

Wife.

Mother of his child.

He nearly roared with triumph.

A wife he didn't want. A child he wasn't ready for.

But damn it, Catie was his now. His forever. And he'd have her tonight. She wasn't resisting. Why shouldn't he have her?

"Chad..." Her voice burrowed against his shoulder.

"Yeah?"

"I...nothing."

"Look, Catie, we don't have to do this."

What the hell was he saying? She was his wife.

"It's okay. I...want you. I've always wanted you. You know that. I'm just sorry."

"Sorry about what? About getting pregnant? Why? It got you what you wanted."

She whipped her head away from his body—he was still holding her—and said, "What I wanted?"

"Me. You've always wanted me."

"Not like this."

"Well, you got me. Now I want to make love to my wife." He placed her on the bed as gently as he could and began to undress her. When her beautiful body had been bared to his view, he ripped his own clothes off and joined her on the bed. He forced his libido to calm. He'd take her, but he'd do it slowly, gently. She deserved that much.

Even though what he wanted at this very moment was to thrust into her and declare to the world that she was his.

A wife he didn't want.

But she was his, damn it, and the world would know it.

He kissed her again. This time gently, but insistently, nibbling across her upper lip and then her lower, running his tongue along the seam of her lips, coaxing her open. When their tongues touched, his groin burst into flames.

Just a kiss from this woman turned him to jelly.

He sucked at her tongue, swirling, coaxing, and then she did it again. She sucked his tongue into her mouth, and he went crazy. He groaned. For a woman who was a virgin a mere few weeks ago, she sure knew how to kiss him into a frenzy.

Her sweet little moans fueled his passion, and he moved on top of her, grinding his erection against her soft curves.

It was going to be so amazing. Sex without a condom. Thirty-two years old, and he'd never experienced the sensation. He'd fuck her with no barrier.

But not yet. Not until she was so soaking wet that she begged him. Then he'd take her, and they'd both soar to the moon.

Chad deepened the kiss, tasting every crevice of her sweet raspberry mouth. He cupped a breast and thumbed one perfect nipple. She wriggled under him, moaning into his mouth. His arousal grew harder. Harder than he'd ever been.

Wife.

Catie was his wife. His. No other man's.

Before he could think, he thrust his hard cock into her moist depth.

God. This is what he'd been missing the last seventeen years? Every ridge, every soft caress of her walls gloved his cock. She moaned beneath him, her voice a soft whisper in the sanctity of their bedroom.

Their bedroom.

He wanted this to be their bedroom.

He withdrew and then thrust again. Only four thrusts and he was coming, spilling inside her.

Inside his wife. Inside his wife where his seed already was being nurtured. Nurtured into a child. His child. His and Catie's.

Would it be little girl who looked just like her beautiful mama?

Or would it be a little boy? A little cowboy who he could teach to rope and to bust broncs. Maybe even ride a bull.

He didn't want to withdraw. He wanted to stay embedded in her—in his wife—forever.

He withdrew.

"Chad?"

"Yeah?"

"Um...which room should I sleep in?"

"Stay here for tonight," he said, wrapping an arm around her waist possessively. "We'll worry about it in the morning."

"But—"

"Just sleep, Catie."

"Uh...well...okay. Good night, Chad."

"Night, rodeo queen."

★ ★ ★

When Chad's breathing had gone steady and shallow, Catie knew he'd fallen asleep. She moved his arm as gently as she could and disengaged herself from his body. She crept silently along the hallway and found a guest room. She fell onto the bed and cried.

"Night, rodeo queen," he'd said.

But she was married now. She was no longer the rodeo queen.

CHAPTER SIXTEEN

"This is wonderful!" Maria Bay grabbed Catie in a hug. "Oh, but why didn't you tell us? We could have given you a proper wedding."

Catie started to speak, but her mother interrupted her. "If only Laurie were alive. She and I so wanted to marry our two families together. It didn't work out with Zach and Angie, but this is so...so..." Maria clamped her hand to her lips and tears welled up in her eyes.

"Mama," Catie said.

"Wayne! Harper!" Maria called through the house. "Shoot. They're out at the barns of course. Or riding with the cattle. You two sit right down, and we'll plan your reception. How about this Saturday? Do you think that's enough time to get it ready and give people enough notice to be here?"

"Mama, please."

"Yes, Catie, what is it?"

Catie inhaled sharply. "Chad and I, that is, this wasn't exactly planned."

"Of course it wasn't planned. You got married in a courthouse without your family. Sometimes young love makes you do strange things. It's still wonderful news. In fact, I'll talk to the attorneys. Maybe there's a way we can combine the properties now. You know, like we tried to do with Zach and Angie. I know Harper's set to inherit Cha Cha, but we could fiddle with the wills and all—"

"Mama!" Catie interrupted. "Please stop this. It's not going to work that way."

"Why not? Laurie and I always dreamed—"

"Maria," Chad said, "Catie and I really need to talk to you. Would you please sit down?"

"Why, yes, of course, Chad. What is it?"

"Chad, let me," Catie said. She took her mother's hand. "Mama, I'm pregnant."

Maria's lips formed a perfect oval.

"It's true. It wasn't planned."

"Oh my, what's your father going to say?"

"He can't say anything, Mama. I know darn well that you were pregnant with Angie when the two of you got married. You weren't in love."

"Caitlyn Anne, that is absolutely not true. I love your father very much."

Catie rolled her eyes. "If you say so. I've never seen much affection pass between the two of you, but it's not for me to say." She cleared her throat. "Chad and I are not in love."

Her face warmed. It wasn't a lie. She might be in love with Chad, but he certainly wasn't in love with her. So "they" were not in love. She glanced at Chad, but he was looking at the floor.

"You see, Mama, Chad insisted that we marry, so his child could have his name."

"Where will you live?"

"With me, of course, Maria," Chad interjected. "Where do you think she'd live?"

"That isn't a marriage."

"It's the marriage we got," Chad said. "Due to circumstances. I'll take good care of Catie."

"Well, of course, I know you will, Chad," Maria said. "But

Catie deserves love and affection."

"Mama, please," Catie said. "You're not making any of this easier. Under the circumstances, I think it'd be better if you don't go off all bonkers and plan a reception. We'll tell the people in town."

"I don't know, Catie. The reception might be a good idea," Chad said.

"What?"

"Well, it'd look pretty strange if we just showed up married with no explanation."

"Uh, we have an explanation, Chad. I'm pregnant."

"Yeah, and people'll find that out soon enough. But it'd be less of a gossip mill if we acted like we were happy about this."

Catie shook her head. "You're kidding me, right? You're worried about gossip?" She scoffed. "This is a farce of a marriage, Chad McCray, and it's no cause for celebration. I don't want a reception. I don't want a party. I don't even want a goddamn wedding announcement."

"Catie, we're married now, and we need to—"

"We don't need to do anything. To hell with Bakersville and its stupid small-town gossip and innuendo. They'll all find out when I go into town tomorrow, to the chamber of commerce."

"Chamber of commerce? What the hell are you talking about, Catie?"

"Yes, Chad, the chamber of commerce. I need to resign as rodeo queen."

"What?"

"You were a judge. Didn't you read the rules? I agreed not to get married during the year of my reign. I broke the rules. Not that it matters. Once they found out I was pregnant, it would have all been over anyway. Not exactly the public image for the sainted rodeo queen."

"Oh, Catie." Maria stood and embraced her daughter.

"Not now, Mama. Please." Catie held her off. "None of this was planned. Just so you know, Chad and I took precautions. This was just an unfortunate accident."

"Catie," Chad began.

"Chad, there is nothing you can say."

"But I need your mother to know... That is, Mrs. Bay, Maria, I... When Catie and I—"

"Chad, please. This is nothing more than an embarrassment," Catie said. "My mother knows full well there are no feelings between us, don't you, Mother?"

"Caitlyn, I think you must be wrong about that," Maria said, "if the two of you made love."

"Had sex, mother. We had sex. That's it. The condom broke."

Chad turned scarlet. Ha. Made him blush. She wouldn't have thought it possible.

"That's all. An accident, pure and simple. Chad and I took precautions. They didn't work."

"Are you sure you don't want the party, honey?"

"Yes, Mama, I'm very sure. Chad, if you'll excuse me, I'm going to do some quick packing, and then I'll drive into town and visit with the chamber of commerce."

"I'll go with you."

"I'd much rather go alone, if you don't mind."

"I'm your husband, Catie. We should both go."

"That's ridiculous. Go on." She shooed him off. "You have a ranch to run. Get on out of here now. My car's here. I'll be fine."

"Uh...all right. Nice to see you, Maria. I'm sorry for how this...you know, about...aw hell. I'm sorry." He put his Stetson on his head and left the Bay house.

"Catie, you weren't very nice to Chad just now," Maria said. "And what do you mean you two aren't in love? You've been mooning after him for years."

"Mama, I was as nice to him as he deserved. He damn near accused me of ripping the condom on purpose yesterday when I told him."

"He didn't!"

"Yes. He did. And I assure you, I had nothing to do with that."

"Oh, of course you didn't. These things just sometimes happen."

"Is that what happened to you and Daddy? With Angie?"

"Oh." She reddened. "I'm embarrassed to say this, Catie, but your father and I... That time, well, we didn't use a condom. We didn't use anything."

"Oh."

"But we had Angie. And then Harper and then you. It hasn't been a failure of a marriage."

"Are you in love?"

"Are you in love with Chad?"

"You know the answer to that question, Mother. And I asked you first."

"No, baby. Your father and I are not in love. We never have been."

"Well, then, Chad and I can make it if you two did. My baby deserves to have a mother and a father in his life. So I'll just live in a loveless marriage."

"But it's not loveless, dear. You love Chad."

"Yes. Yes, I do. But he doesn't love me. And I doubt he ever will." She turned toward the stairway. "I've got packing to do."

★ ★ ★

Why the hell wasn't Catie happy? She'd wanted him. She'd made no bones about it. He got into his pickup, headed to Zach's, and then remembered he and Dusty were out of town and Sean was staying with Dallas and Annie. He changed directions and headed toward his oldest brother's house.

Surprisingly, both Dallas and Annie were at home. He figured Dallas might be out with the stock and Annie might be in town at her vet's office.

"Are you kidding?" Annie said. "With three kids this week, I canceled all my appointments, though I'm still on call."

"Me? I just came in for lunch," Dallas said. "You want to join us?"

"Not hungry."

Dallas guffawed. "That's gotta be a first. Come sit down with us anyway. Bea's already got the kids taken care of."

"Okay. I need to talk to you."

"What's up?" Annie asked.

Chad sat, and Annie put a sandwich in front of him.

"Well, I guess I'll just come right out and say it. I married Catie Bay yesterday."

Dallas jumped from his chair. "You what?"

"You heard me."

"Chad, that's wonderful news," Annie said.

"It's not exactly as wonderful as you might think."

"Why on earth not? And why'd you do it yesterday?" She swatted him. "Dallas and I could have stood up for you."

"She's pregnant, Annie."

"Aw, man," Dallas said. "How the hell did that happen?"

"The same way the twins happened, I suspect," Chad said. "Jesus, Dallas."

"I mean, didn't you learn your lesson—"

"Don't bring that up." Chad gritted his teeth. "I took every necessary precaution."

"Then what happened?"

"Catie says the condom broke."

"What do you mean, 'Catie says.'"

"Says she saw it by the wastebasket the next morning, after I'd already gone out to work. It had a tear in it."

"Well, you put it on, didn't you?"

"Uh, yeah, the first couple of times, anyway."

"Couple of times?" Annie shrieked. "What the hell's been going on, Chad?"

"It was... Hell, I don't know. I can't talk about this."

"I understand," Dallas said. "It's private. But you took precautions. It sounds like this was just an unfortunate accident. It happens."

"Not to me. At least not anymore."

"Clearly it does."

"Yeah. So I married her."

"The great and single Chad McCray, brought to the altar by a little rodeo queen." Annie laughed.

"Ha. I guess she's no longer our rodeo queen, brother."

"Yeah, that's what she said. She's gonna go by the chamber of commerce today and resign."

"Too bad. She was a fine choice," Dallas said.

"Oh, she must be heartbroken," Annie said.

"Heartbroken?" Chad shook his head, bewildered. "Are

you serious? My life has turned upside down, and you're worried about Catie's status as rodeo queen?"

"Chad, think of what this is doing to her. She's only twenty-one, and she's going to be a mother. And now she's a wife. A wife to a man who only married her out of obligation."

"I didn't marry her out of obligation!"

"So you're saying you have feelings for her?"

"I'm saying... Hell, I don't know what I'm saying. This is none of your goddamn business anyway." He stood and pushed his chair under the table as though it were poison. "I don't know why I came over here."

"You may not have feelings for her, Chad," Annie said, "but you know darn well she has feelings for you. She always has."

"Schoolgirl crush."

"Schoolgirl crush? She's twenty-one years old."

"She's worshiped me for years. She doesn't know any better. It's habit."

Annie threw her hands in the air. "Are you hearing yourself?"

"You're not making any sense, Chad," Dallas said. "No matter how the events were set in motion, you know Ma's smiling from her grave. She's been wanting our two families to marry together since the Zach and Angie debacle six years ago."

"Yeah, well, I wasn't planning on it having anything to do with me."

"Uncle Chad!"

He looked up and Sean came running in. Chad scooped the boy into his arms. "Partner, shouldn't you be taking your after lunch nap?"

"Naps are for girls."

"And little boys," Annie said. "Here, Chad, I'll take him."

"Nah, it's okay. Can I take him outside for a few minutes?"

He looked at his nephew, again amazed at how much he resembled his mother. Hardly any of Zach in him, except for those crazy light blue eyes.

Dusty couldn't have more children. Cancer therapy when she was younger had all but destroyed her reproductive system. Sean had been a pleasant surprise and a blessing for her and Zach. Though another pregnancy was possible, it was damned improbable.

Yet he, Chad, could have all the children he wanted. Now he had one on the way. One he didn't want. With a wife he didn't want.

Gone was his old way of life.

"So when're we goin' fishin'?" Sean asked.

"Well, critter, I don't know. You know how busy your pa and Uncle Dallas and I are with running this ranch. Why don't we make a date of it once your ma and pa are back in town, okay?"

"Okay!" Sean wrapped his arms around Chad and gave him a sloppy kiss on the cheek.

What a great kid. And he was the apple of his daddy's eye.

Would Chad feel that way about Catie's baby? He whipped his head backward, dislodging his nephew.

Catie's baby.

It wasn't just Catie's baby.

It was *his* baby.

He curved his lips slightly upward and stroked Sean's baby soft blond hair.

His baby.

He'd be there for this one. In more ways than just his money. He wouldn't just be a father. He'd be a daddy.

CHAPTER SEVENTEEN

The meeting with the Bakersville alderman had been uneventful. Now Catie was loading her clothes into the closet in the guestroom where she had spent the night in Chad's house.

She had no idea where Chad was, and she didn't righteously care.

What a big ol' lie. She cared. She'd cared for seventeen years, and she wasn't about to stop caring now. She sighed, sat down on the bed, and touched her tummy.

"It'll be okay, little one," she said. "You'll have a mommy and daddy who love you. And a mommy who loves your daddy, even if he'll never love her back. I promise."

The phone rang. A football phone. This was her room now and that would be the first thing to go. She picked it up. Chad's home phone. Heck, her home phone now.

"Hello. McCray residence."

"Yes, hello. I need to speak to Chad McCray please."

"I'm sorry. He's out right now. May I take a message?"

"Who's this?"

The woman's tone was a bit on the snotty side. Well, Catie could give it right back.

"This is Chad's wife. Who's this?"

"Wife?"

"Yes. I'm Caitlyn McCray. And you are?"

Click.

HELEN HARDT

Stupid football phone didn't have caller ID. Catie raced to the kitchen where she hit the history button. *Rhine, L.*

Well, Rhine, L., whatever you wanted Chad for, forget it. He's mine now.

★ ★ ★

Catie sighed as she drove out to the nearest stable, where Ladybird had been housed.

"Hi there, ma'am." A dark and handsome man tipped his Stetson to her. "Can I help you?"

"I'm just going to visit my horse."

"I'm Rafe Grayhawk, ma'am, foreman in charge of this particular stable. You the owner of that pretty new mare brought in this morning?"

"If you mean the dark chestnut, yes."

"That's some mighty fine horseflesh, ma'am."

"Please," Catie said, "you don't have to call me ma'am."

Rafe's black eyes burned into her. His skin was a light bronze color, and when he took off his Stetson, she saw that his pitch-black hair was pulled back into an untidy low ponytail behind his neck. Strands of ebony silk flitted about his chiseled face in the summer breeze, gleaming with sapphire highlights in the afternoon sun.

"Then it would help if I knew your name, honey."

He smiled, and she could almost see him wearing a Native American headdress, and...not much else. He was a beautiful man.

Catie swallowed, but didn't answer.

"If we're boarding your horse here, you and I'll get to know each other quite a bit better," Rafe said. "I'll be the one making sure she gets what she needs. What's her name?"

"Ladybird."

"Well, she's sure a beaut."

"Yeah." Catie nodded. "That she is."

"So, sweetheart…"

Despite her love for Chad, Catie's heart lurched at the endearment. Nice to know there might be a man around here who wanted her. One who wasn't stuck with her out of some misguided obligation.

"Yeah?"

He chuckled. "You still haven't told me your name."

"Oh." She cleared her throat. "I'm sorry. It's Catie."

Rafe moved closer and pushed a strand of dark hair out of Catie's eye. His touch was warm and pleasant. Not hot and passionate, like Chad's.

"It's this wind," she said. "My hair won't stay in one place. It's a real pain."

"Not so much a pain," Rafe said. "You look real pretty, Catie. All rosy-cheeked and windblown. I bet you want to take your horse on a ride, don't you?"

"Yeah. I'd like that." A ride with Ladybird would be the perfect salve for her ailing heart, to take her mind off of Chad and Rhine, L. and this farce of a marriage she had agreed to.

"Well, then, Miss Catie," Rafe said, holding out his hand to her, "I'll be right glad to take you into the stables and get her saddled up, for a small price."

Price?

"Uh, what do you want?"

"Your name, honey."

"I told you my name. It's Catie."

"The last name, pretty lady. Catie what?"

The husky voice that came out of nowhere surprised her. "Catie McCray."

"Hey, Chad," Rafe said. "Where'd you come from?"

"I get around, Grayhawk." He draped his arm possessively around Catie's shoulders and pulled her close, jostling her so hard that she winced. "From now on, keep your paws off my wife."

"Your wife? Hell, I didn't know, Chad. Since when do you have a wife?"

"Since yesterday. If I see you sniffing around her again, you can find yourself another job."

"Chad," Catie said, "he was just going to help me saddle Ladybird for a ride."

"I know how these hands are, Catie. They can't keep their hands to themselves around a beautiful woman. You stay clear of them."

"That's the most ridiculous thing I've ever heard. I grew up around ranch hands. They're fine."

"Look, Chad. She's your wife, I get it. I was just gettin' to know her, that's all."

"Go on and do your job, Grayhawk. I'll saddle Catie's horse."

"As you say, boss."

Once Rafe had left, Chad dragged Catie into the stable and pushed her against the wall. The faint smell of horse manure mixed with the fresh scent of hay assaulted Catie's nose. Until Chad's face came within an inch of hers, and then all she could smell was him. Spicy Chad. Musky Chad. Manly Chad. Her husband. She inhaled deeply.

"What the hell do you think you're doing?" he demanded. His cheeks reddened and his nostrils flared. Catie flinched. He was angry. Really angry. Possibly more angry than when she'd told him she was pregnant.

"I... I was going to take a ride. I'm...a little stressed Chad. I—"

He silenced her with a punishing kiss. His lips clamped onto hers, forcing her mouth open, his tongue thrusting inside. She gasped, trying to breathe through her nose, but he was holding her so close, so tight. She pushed at his chest and tried to free herself, but it was no use. He held her against the wall, against his body. She was trapped.

Chad finally ripped his mouth away, and they both took deep breaths.

"What...is wrong...with you?" Catie's words came out between gasps. "I just wanted to see Lady—"

"Shut up!" He crushed his mouth to hers again.

The kiss was gentler this time, though not by much. He swept into her mouth like a tidal wave, thrusting with his tongue and then retreating, while he simultaneously thrust his hips and ground them into hers, mimicking what he was doing to her mouth with his tongue. What she instinctively knew he wanted to do with his cock.

Would do with his cock. He was already unsnapping her jeans.

She tried to escape his kiss, but to no avail. He held her fast. Her slim form was no match for his musculature. He held her fast against his broad hard chest as he unzipped her jeans and plunged his long, thick fingers inside. She gasped into his mouth, and he groaned. She felt, more than heard it, a faint rumble in her mouth, against her breasts. She began to writhe as he touched her, grinding into his hand.

He broke their kiss with a loud smack.

"God, you're so fucking wet." He shuddered against her. "You like it when I touch you there, don't you, sugar?"

Catie's breath puffed against Chad's cheek. His words were a husky whisper against her sweaty neck.

"Don't you?" he said again.

"Y-Yes. You know I do."

"Why'd you leave my bed this morning?" He nibbled on her neck. Tiny little nips that turned into bites. They stung. A little bit pleasure, a little bit pain.

"I..."

"I woke up and you were gone." He bit her earlobe. "I wanted you next to me."

"But this isn't..."

She lost her train of thought for few seconds as he sucked on the spot below her ear that made her crazy. She sighed, and then gasped as he bit her neck again. Still his fingers worked her. She squirmed as tiny sparks erupted on her skin.

She inhaled, and then answered his question. "It's not a real marriage."

He backed off a little at that. He looked straight at her, his dark eyes scalding hot. He grabbed her hand, led it to his crotch, and rubbed it over his denim-clad arousal. "Does this feel real to you, sugar?"

"It... It was never a question of that." She closed her eyes he slid his fingers through her folds and pushed one inside her. She gasped. The invasion was so sweet, so right.

"Tell me, sugar. How does *that* feel?"

"Good, Chad. So good."

He pushed his finger farther into her. "That?"

"Heaven," she rasped against his cheek, kissing it, letting the day's growth of his beard prickle her lips.

"Let me tell you something, Catie McCray."

He helped her unbuckle and unsnap his jeans. Nibbling on her ear, he pushed her jeans down, and then his own. When the hard head of his cock pressed against her wet flesh, she shuddered.

"You're mine. All mine." He pushed his cock into her wet channel. "You're not for Grayhawk or anyone else around here, you got that?"

She gasped as he withdrew and pushed into her again.

"Answer me, damn it." His voice was raw. Untamed.

"Wh-What?"

"Who do you belong to, Catie?"

"You, Chad."

"Whose bed are you going to sleep in from now on?" His thrusts became faster, more urgent.

"Y-Yours. Only yours."

He plunged into her again, at the same time as his mouth came down on hers and assaulted her. They kissed in a frenzy of tongues and teeth, devouring each other, as though they'd been starved for years, centuries.

When he broke the kiss, Catie drew a deep breath, her passions rising, her skin tingling.

"That's right, sugar. Come for me." Chad's fingers touched her swollen flesh as he continued to pound into her. "For me. Only for me."

At his command, she shattered, her body quaking as the rapture took her through a kaleidoscope of colors and shapes. From somewhere outside her body, she heard her own voice—or a husky, low imitation of it—echoing Chad's name.

As she started her descent, Chad pushed harder, stronger, flooding her with new and vibrant sensations.

"Damn, you're even tighter after you come, baby. Give me one...more...ah!"

He thrust into her so deep, that for a moment she thought they'd become one being. His whole body trembled against her, perspiration trickling down his cheeks and neck, dripping onto her neck, trailing down between her breasts. He stayed there for a precious moment, holding her, leaning into her, before he pulled away and pulled up his boxers and jeans.

He pulled a blue bandana out of his pocket and handed it to her. "Here," he said. "Clean yourself up."

Then he left the stable.

What? Catie stood dumbfounded, her jeans and panties still around her ankles, Chad's hanky hanging limply from her fist.

This was really it?

Her cheeks heating, she wiped the evidence of their lovemaking from herself with a few quick swipes, pulled up her jeans, and fastened them.

Again, he'd taken her to the stars.

He'd made love to her with a passion so fierce, she wasn't sure it was real. In her inexperience, she had nothing to compare it to. Was it always like this?

He'd said she was his.

His.

But he hadn't said the three words she so desperately needed to hear. Instead, he'd left her, like always.

She slid down the wall, the splintery wood scraping her back through her cotton shirt, into a sitting position. Pulling her knees up, she wrapped her arms around them and fell to the side, onto the hay-covered floor. She lay there, in a fetal position, waiting for the tears to come.

They didn't. Was she truly all cried out over Chad?

She didn't know how long she stayed in that position. Eventually she felt a nudge on her arm. "Hey there, Ms. McCray."

She opened her eyes and stared into the black orbs of Rafe Grayhawk.

"You need any help with anything?"

Catie bolted upward, sniffing. Thank God, the tears hadn't come, or her face would be pink and splotchy.

"I think your husband can afford a better place for you to nap, sweetheart," Rafe said, extending his hand.

Catie took his hand gratefully and stood up. "I must have fallen asleep. Chad and I... We had a long day yesterday."

"Thought you were gonna take that pretty mare on a ride?"

"Yeah. Yeah. I am."

"I'll saddle her up."

"Chad said—"

"I know what Chad said, Ms. McCray."

He winked, and she couldn't help smiling at the handsome ranch hand.

"I'll mind my Ps and Qs, don't you worry."

"Please."

"Okay, I'll leave. No harm done."

"No." She shook her head. "I meant, please call me Catie."

"Not sure the boss would approve."

"I don't care. I didn't ask for his opinion on the matter."

Catie brushed the dirt and hay off her thighs. To hell with what Chad said. She and Rafe weren't doing anything wrong. He was helping her, that's all. She touched his forearm—as hard and sinewy as Chad's, though it didn't induce the sparks on her skin the way Chad's did.

"I'd love your help saddling Ladybird, if you don't mind. After all, you need to get to know her now."

"True enough," Rafe said with a cocky grin and walked toward Ladybird's stall. "If I had an hour or two free, I'd saddle up my bronc and go along with you. Course we know the boss'd frown on that."

Catie smiled. This young man was kind and easy to talk to. So much easier to talk to than her distant husband, who wanted to love her body, but not the rest of her.

"No doubt he would," Catie agreed, "but I'll tell you what."

Rafe turned back around and met her gaze. "What?"

. She winked. "We'll just keep it between us, okay?"

His lazy grin lit up his handsome features. "Darlin', that's about the best idea I've heard this year." He turned and continued saddling Ladybird.

★ ★ ★

Catie rode Ladybird to Annie and Dallas's house. Later, sitting with Annie over herb tea, Catie spilled her guts.

"I don't know what to do," she said, after pouring out the story of her and Chad, the baby, and the bedroom situation. "He seems to want me, but yet he doesn't. This whole baby thing—" She patted her belly. "I want this child. More than anything. But as much as I love Chad, I never wanted it to be like this. It really was an accident, Annie."

"I know it was," Annie said, consoling. "And so does Chad."

"Does he really?"

"Yeah. He does. Don't you worry about that." Annie

freshened Catie's tea.

"This isn't the kind of marriage I wanted."

"I know, hon."

Catie sighed. "But it's what I got. Do you think he might ever love me?"

"Oh, Catie." Annie reached out and touched Catie's forearm. "I think he already does. He just doesn't know it yet."

Catie jerked backward. "You can't be serious."

"I sure am. Do you think, for one minute, that Chad McCray is the kind of guy to do anything he doesn't want to do?"

"Well...no."

"So you think he married you when he didn't want to, out of sole obligation?"

"Well, I think he's concerned about his child. He wanted him or her to have his name. And the advantage of being a McCray."

Annie shook her head and chuckled. "You've known Chad lots longer than I have, Catie, but you sure can be blind when it comes to him."

"Love is blind, as they say," Catie said.

"Blind, yes. But deaf and dumb, too? Do you really think Chad would have dragged you down the aisle just to give his kid a name? I'm not sure you know him at all."

"Of course I know him."

"I didn't mean that as an insult, hon. That's just the truth of it. You had him on a pedestal all those star-crossed teen years, and then you left for four years. Things change, Catie. People change. But Chad didn't change. *You* did."

"Me?"

"Yes. Chad was always a womanizer. You know that.

Never serious. Do you think you're the first woman to ever claim she was having his child?"

"But—"

"But nothing. He's gorgeous, he's rich, and women have been falling all over him for damn near fifteen years. A few have come out of the woodwork, claiming to be pregnant."

"They have?"

"Only a few, but yeah. And you're his first wife. What do you think of that?"

"What about the others?"

"None of them were telling the truth."

"But I am."

"I know you are. And so does Chad."

"How did he know the rest of them weren't?"

"He hired his PI friend, Larry something or other, to track down the truth on them."

"Why didn't he have me checked out?"

Annie smiled, rubbing Catie's forearm in a motherly manner. "Why don't *you* tell *me*?"

★ ★ ★

Later, Catie continued to fold her clothes and put them away in the guestroom where she had spent her first night as Mrs. Chad McCray. If he wanted her in his bed, he was going to have to love her first. She only intended to share a bed with a husband who loved her. She may not be able to resist his lovemaking, but she sure as hell didn't have to kowtow to his demands. She'd be friends with Rafe Grayhawk, too, if she wanted, and any of the other hands.

Once she finished filling up the guestroom closet, she

dragged her computer in from the car and decided to set it up in Chad's office. She walked in his nicely decorated den and sat down at his desk.

An instant message came up on his computer. From Lindabelle.

L: You there?
Lindabelle. Rhine, L. Could it be?
She touched the keyboard.

C: Yeah.
L: I talked to your wife earlier.
C: Wife?
L: Yeah, wife. There's some woman in your house answering your phone, claiming to be your wife.
C: I guess I got married.

Is that something Chad would have said? Catie wasn't sure. She hardly knew her husband.

L: You did?
C: Yeah. What do you want anyway?
L: Congratulations. She seemed real sweet. Didn't know where you were though. Seems weird, if you're newlyweds.
C: I run a ranch. No one knows where I am all the time.

Good answer, Catie.

L: Have you told her about our arrangement?

Catie gasped. What arrangement? She started shuffling

papers around on Chad's desk. *Rhine, L. Rhine, L.* Chad's filing cabinet. She'd have to look there.

Ding. Another IM.

L: Well, have you?
C: Not yet.
L: Don't you think Mrs. Chad McCray has a right to know where her husband's money goes every month?

What?

C: I'll tell her when I get to it.
L: Okay.
C: This isn't any of your business, L.

She took a shot. Assumed this was *Rhine, L.* Rhine. Her name was probably Linda from her IM ID Lindabelle.

L: Maybe not. But I do care about you, Chad. If this marriage of yours is going to work, you need to tell her about Jack.

Catie stopped reading. Jack? Her pulse raced. Her afternoon conversation with Annie raced through her mind. Several women had come around claiming to be pregnant, trying to trap Chad.

Rhine, L.

Jack.

She got up and yanked open Chad's filing cabinet looking for anything. Any type of clue.

Finally, it appeared. A file folder. Rhine, Linda. Inside

was only one paper. The results of a DNA test naming Chad McCray as the father of Linda Rhine's son, Jack. According to the birth date, the child was over four years old.

Ding. The IM again. Catie didn't bother reading it. She couldn't. Her vision was clouded with tears. She typed in a message quickly.

C: I have a meeting. I've got to go.

Then she turned away from the computer and looked down at her belly.

"Well, sweetheart," she said aloud, gulping through sobs, "it looks like you already have a big brother."

She needed some answers. She looked into the file folder again and found Linda Rhine's address in Utah. About a day's drive. Well, she had nothing better to do. No rodeo queen duties.

Nice day for a road trip.

Or night, rather. The sun was already setting.

She threw some clothes into a duffle and plugged the address into the GPS on her phone.

She'd planned to meet Harper later and talk about getting her other stock over to one of Chad's barns this evening. That could wait a few days. Right now, she had a rival to face.

At four in the morning, Catie arrived in Podunk, Utah. Actually, Applewood, Utah, but it made Bakersville look like a thriving metropolis. Of course, it was the middle of the night. Perhaps it would look like civilization in the morning. There was only one motel in town, and they luckily had a vacancy, though she had to ring the bell ten times before someone came to help her. Finally, an older man, rubbing his sleep-filled eyes, came to the counter and booked her into a room. Sleep came as soon as her head hit the pillow, her eyes swollen from crying.

★ ★ ★

Where the hell was Catie?

Chad lay awake, Marnie snuggled by his feet. The minutes crept by on his digital clock. He'd watched two o'clock come and go, and then three, and now four. Damn. Anxiety gnawed at him. She wasn't at home. He'd called the Bays earlier. He couldn't call them again. He'd just worry them. She wasn't with Dallas and Annie, and Zach and Dusty were out of town.

He got up, paced, and went down to his office. He couldn't sleep anyway. Might as well get some work done. He took out his business account, wrote out some invoices, paid some bills, and went to settle some of his personal accounts. The grocery bill, the gas for the giant propane tank that fed his house, water, electric, septic system.

And Linda and Jack needed to be paid.

He had no legal obligation to the woman and her son, but he wanted to help them, especially after hearing what she'd gone through with her parents. He'd have to tell Catie. Where the hell was she?

He'd felt a loss when he woke up the previous morning and she wasn't next to him. He'd pattered down the hallway and found her sleeping soundly in one of his guest rooms. That told him how she felt about him. So much for her schoolgirl crush.

Yet she responded to him today in the stable, when he'd taken her roughly like a selfish bastard. He was sorry for it. But when he'd seen Grayhawk with his hands on his woman...

His woman.

His wife.

Tonight she hadn't come to his bed like he'd asked. Aw

hell, like he'd *demanded*. What had he become? What was it
about this one little woman that turned him into a feral beast?
Well, he hadn't exactly been nice to her about the whole baby
thing. He knew she wasn't pulling a stunt on him. Warmth
crept up his skin, making it tingle. Truth be told, he *wanted*
Catie's baby. A little person who was part Catie and part Chad.

He cared for Catie. Maybe he didn't love her yet, but he
sure as hell felt a lot more for her than he had for any other
woman.

An urge to barge into the guest room and force her back
into his bed overwhelmed him, but he resisted. He scribbled
out a note to leave on the counter in the kitchen. He had to go
out of town on business and would be in Denver overnight.
He'd leave before she was up in the morning. He checked the
coffee machine to make sure Brenda had set it for six a.m.
Yep, good. He left the note for Catie and then made his way to
his bedroom and flopped onto his big empty bed. He inhaled
Catie's scent on the pillow. Mmm, raspberries and lime. His
wife. His wife who should be in his bed. Though he was hard
as granite, he was determined to leave her alone. He hadn't
been easy on her.

One thing was for sure, though. When he got back from
Denver, they'd have a serious discussion about their marriage.
This was going to work, damn it.

★ ★ ★

Catie took a deep breath before she knocked on the door of
the modest house on Cherrytree Street in the small town of
Applewood, Utah.

It was Saturday, and she hoped Rhine, L would be home.

Sure enough, a pretty blond woman answered, smiling.

"Yes, may I help you?"

"Are you Linda Rhine?"

"I suppose that depends on who wants to know."

"I'm Caitlyn Bay...I mean McCray. Caitlyn McCray."

The woman's smile faded. "Oh. You're Chad's wife."

"Yes. May I come in?"

She sighed and her cheeks reddened. "Of course. Yes. What can I do for you?" She held the door open. "I'm sure this isn't really what you're used to."

Catie forced her lips upward. No reason not to be pleasant. "Don't be silly. It's lovely." Small and modest, the home was clean and decorated beautifully. Linda clearly loved plants. Greenery adorned every table and nook.

"Is—" Catie cleared her throat. "Is your son here?"

Linda fidgeted with her hands. "Yeah. He's up in his room playing."

"I'd love to meet him."

"Of course. I'll go get him. Please make yourself at home."

Catie sat down in a hunter-green recliner. Tiny hooves danced in her tummy. She swallowed, forcing back nausea. So Chad had a son. No big deal, right? He wouldn't be the first man to knock up a woman out of wedlock. Heck, he'd done it twice now.

Why hadn't he told her? Why hadn't Annie? Instead, she'd looked Catie straight in the eye and said Chad had checked out all the women who claimed to be pregnant with his child.

Linda returned with a pretty little blond boy who looked nothing like Chad. He was a dead ringer for Linda, though, so he could still be Chad's kid. Heck, she herself didn't resemble Wayne at all.

"He's very handsome, Linda."

"Thank you."

"He's about the same age as Chad's nephew, Sean."

"I don't know about Chad's nephew. But Jack's four."

Catie smiled at the little boy, and he smiled back.

"So Chad told you about us, huh? Last night, when I spoke to him, he said he hadn't yet."

"We don't have any secrets," Catie said, wishing to the stars that she spoke the truth. "I wanted to come up here to meet you and his—" The words stuck in her throat like peanut butter. "Jack." She'd almost said son, but couldn't.

"Oh. Can I offer you anything?"

"No. I won't stay long."

Fifteen minutes of small talk later, Catie left.

★ ★ ★

Catie hadn't come home.

Chad's stomach churned. Was she all right? Was the baby all right?

He'd called Wayne and Maria, and then the police. No one knew where she was. Her car was gone though, so she probably hadn't been taken. Then again, someone could have held her at gunpoint.

Chad shuffled through her bedroom like a madman, looking for clues. Nothing. Hmm...she'd set up her computer recently. He ran down the stairwell and into his office. He opened each drawer of his desk, of his credenza. Nothing again. He flew to his file cabinet, his heart stampeding, and opened each drawer, searching for something, anything.

He found it.

The file on Linda Rhine had been replaced in the cabinet backwards.

Damn! Catie must have found out about Linda's son. Would she have gone to see Linda?

Chad cursed to himself. Damn those conniving people!

He didn't mind taking care of the kid. The poor boy didn't have anyone else. But damned if he'd let this situation jeopardize his marriage.

He shook his head.

Did he want this marriage after all?

Catie's image—her soft mahogany hair, her big brown eyes, her slender and shapely legs that went on forever—eased into his consciousness. Had her image always been there? Since she'd stumbled back into his life a few weeks ago, she hadn't left his thoughts for more than a minute at a time. His mind whirled to that fateful night in the gazebo four years ago. God, he'd wanted her, would have given his fortune for one taste of her innocent sweetness. She'd said she hadn't yet kissed a boy.

He'd reminded her he was no boy.

She'd been a kid then—just turned eighteen. A kid in a beautiful woman's body. He'd summoned every speck of willpower he possessed to reject her.

Now Hurricane Catie had returned, wreaking havoc in his life.

Fuck.

He'd never been so happy.

Love.

How hadn't he recognized it? Had he been so adamant about not making a commitment that he'd been ready to let her walk out of his life?

Her beauty, her intelligence, her love and knowledge of horses, her clumsiness—everything about her touched his soul. God bless that ripped condom. Without it, he'd have let her go.

Determination rose within him. He'd find her and he'd keep her. Somehow, he'd convince her that his love for her was real.

CHAPTER EIGHTEEN

Catie's research online at the local library and hall of records hadn't turned up anything important. Jack Rhine had been born in Salt Lake City a little over four years ago. Linda had lived in this little town of Applewood her whole life. She worked as a secretary for a local realtor. She seemed to be well-liked in town. Her son stayed at the local daycare center during the week. Linda's mother and stepfather, Dorothy and Blake Smith, lived nearby. No mention of Chad McCray anywhere.

Would he deny his own son?

Catie shook her head as she closed the last document on the library computer. Perhaps she really didn't know this man who she'd married. This man she'd loved her entire life. This man whose child she carried.

Exhausted, she plunked her head on the keyboard. Sadness overwhelmed her, trickled through every vein in her body, yet strangely her eyes produced no tears. Was she truly all cried out over Chad McCray?

She sighed. The hour was late, and a long drive home awaited her. She stood and pressed her hands onto the keyboard. A sharp pain lanced through her abdomen. She inhaled and looked down.

A small spot of crimson glared up from the white plastic chair.

Not the baby. I can't lose my baby.

The tears that had refused to fall only minutes ago now gushed forth like torrential rains.

Help. She needed medical help. She tried to walk to the counter, but a haze filled her head and her legs wobbled. Cramps pierced into her tummy.

"Ma'am?" An elderly librarian rushed to her. "Do you need help? Oh! You're bleeding. Let's get you to a doctor."

Mama's been through this. I want Mama. I want my baby.

"Please, I just want to go home."

"Nonsense. It's after hours, but I'll call Dr. Weinstein. We'll go to his urgent care clinic. He won't mind. Small-town doctors are used to nighttime emergencies."

Before Catie could protest, the librarian had helped her into a brown sedan.

Catie's weeping continued. How could this have happened? At least Chad was off the hook. He'd no longer be shackled to a wife he didn't want, a baby he didn't want. Hell, he hadn't wanted Linda's either. If he had, he'd have married her and taken care of her and the kid.

Yet he *had* married Catie. Did that mean anything? Nah. He hadn't been happy about it. Maybe Linda had refused him. If so, she had strength Catie didn't possess. She wiped at her eyes with the hanky the kind librarian had given her. Chad would have married Linda. Clearly, he was taking care of their child.

Soon they arrived at the clinic. A nurse ushered Catie in, took her to an urgent care exam room, and started an IV.

"I'm giving you something for the pain, Dr. Weinstein's orders," the nurse said. "He'll be here soon."

Catie sighed and regarded the needle in her hand. Soon the cramping would lessen thanks to the drugs dripping into her veins. Too bad they couldn't do anything for her emotional pain.

She lay on the uncomfortable bed and waited for the doctor to come in and give her the news she already knew.

She had lost Chad's baby.

She had lost Chad.

★ ★ ★

Because she was so early in her pregnancy, she didn't need a D and C. She had expelled what little tissue there was naturally. The doctor released her later in the evening with a prescription for antibiotics and pain pills and instructions to take it easy. No sex for four weeks. Didn't matter. The only man she wanted to have sex with didn't want her, and she was done having sex with men who didn't want her.

Should she have called him? Nah. She shook her head. He didn't care. If Annie had left, Dallas would have moved heaven and earth to find her. Ditto Zach and Dusty. But not little brother Chad. He didn't care that his wife had been missing for twenty-four hours. Now that the baby was gone, no reason existed to prolong this sham of a marriage.

The kind nurse drove her to the library to retrieve her car, followed her to the hotel, and made her promise not to drive until morning, when the pain medication had left her system.

It was a promise Catie did not keep.

She packed up her overnight bag and quickly rummaged through her purse. Yes, her procrastinating nature had paid off—she hadn't yet removed her passport and put it in the safe. She should call her parents. Even Chad. He'd have told them she was gone by now. But she couldn't. She wasn't ready to talk yet. Besides, they'd find her easily enough. She hadn't covered her tracks. She'd call them all when she reached her destination. For she wasn't going home. She was going straight to Salt Lake City, to the airport.

Back to France.

Away from Chad.

She had friends in Europe who would welcome her. She'd already called and told Dominic that she was coming. As soon as she had her arrival information, she'd text it.

★ ★ ★

The verge of insanity niggled at the back of Chad's neck like fingers scraping a chalkboard. A quick phone call to Linda had confirmed Catie had visited, but Linda had no idea where she was staying or if she was still in Applewood. He found her at a local motel, but had come up empty-handed when he tried to call her room. No answer. No answer on her cell either. Was she deliberately avoiding him?

He could drive to Applewood, but that would take hours. His PI buddy, Larry Parks, could easily track Catie down in less than half the time. He put in the call and wasn't surprised when Larry called back in less than an hour.

"What's the good news, Lar?"

"I found her, Chad."

"Yeah? Where is she?"

"She's—" Larry cleared his throat.

"What? Tell me!"

"She's on a flight to Paris."

Had a Taser gun hit him? Chad's body suddenly went numb. "What?"

"She's on a flight to Paris."

He shook his head, his body tingling. "But why?"

"I can't get into her head, Chad. I don't have a clue why she's on a flight to Paris, but it may have something to do with the fact that she paid a visit to a doctor last evening."

Fear gripped him. "A doctor? Why? Is she okay?"

"Yes, yes, she's fine," Larry assured.

Chad sat down limply. "Thank God."

"There's something I need to tell you though."

He stood up again, his pulse thundering inside his ears. "What is it?"

"She lost the baby, Chad."

"Damn." A cannonball settled in Chad's gut. Anger, sadness, worry cascaded over him. He threw his phone down and then picked it up again. "You still there, Lar?"

"Yeah, I'm here."

"What's her flight number?"

He scribbled the information on a legal pad, thanked Larry before he hung up, and made a quick call to his travel agent.

Within five hours, Chad was on his way to Paris.

A flirty flight attendant brought him wine and pillows and helped him lean his seat back when the pilot turned off the cabin lights.

"Can I get you anything else, sir?" she asked. "A blanket, maybe?"

"No, honey, I'm perfectly comfortable," he said. No one sat in the seat next to him, so he had the first class row to himself. He leaned into the soft, though not comfortable, headrest and closed his eyes.

Catie, I'm coming for you, he thought. *I love you. I've loved you for so long that I can't imagine not loving you. Somehow I've always known it would be you. I feel lost when you're gone. I feel like a part of me's missing. I've always known, Catie, I've always known...*

As he drifted into slumber, a fateful evening four years earlier drifted into his mind.

"Hi there, Chad."

"Hey, Catie. Happy birthday. You sure look pretty tonight."

"You actually noticed?"

"I've been noticing for a while now. You've grown into a pretty girl."

"Woman, Chad. I'm eighteen. I've grown into a pretty woman."

She walked closer, her breath coming in short puffs. A silky green sundress sheathed her nubile body. Warm mahogany tresses fell over faintly freckled shoulders. Kissable shoulders... Damn, she was a beautiful woman. Girl, he corrected his thoughts. Catie was a girl. He willed his heart to slow before he spoke.

"Eighteen ain't a woman in my book, little bit."

"Why do you call me that?" she asked coyly.

"You know why. When you were four and I was fifteen, working at your house with Angie on a school project. You kept bugging us, and Angie bribed you with cookies just to leave us alone for a little bit." He chuckled. "Course you always came back for more."

"Well"—Catie edged closer to him—"cookies have always been my downfall. Good thing I'm not prone to weight gain." She backed away for a moment and stuck out her chest, the soft clingy satin making her pert nipples apparent through the fabric.

Chad's groin tightened. For a moment, he imagined biting one of those hard little nubs right through the green satin.

"What do you think? Do I need to lose any weight?"

Chad gulped, silently he hoped. "I have no opinion on the matter."

What a crock. He had an opinion on the matter. Not one change needed to be made to that perfect young body. Had her legs always been that long? Damned if they didn't go on forever. The gift that keeps on giving...

Catie leaned over the redwood railing. "Angie and Cal Tucker used to make out here in high school. I'd sneak over and spy on them."

"What were you? Five or six then?"

"About five. I always thought, someday, I'd make out with the man of my dreams here too."

"Cal Tucker was hardly the man of Angie's dreams, little bit."

"Oh, I don't know."

"She was never the woman of his dreams, that's for sure. He was after anything in a skirt back in high school."

She batted her eyes. Big brown doe eyes. His breath caught.

"You're one to talk."

He couldn't help a chuckle. "Never claimed to be a saint, little bit."

She sauntered toward him, her narrow hips swaying just enough to drive him crazy.

"Tell me, Chad." She licked her ruby lips. "Do I look eighteen to you? Do I look like a woman? Or do you still see a little girl?"

Chad closed his eyes. "Why are you doing this, Catie?"

A whisper of skin grazed his chin. Her fingertips.

"Open your eyes, Chad McCray. Open them and look at me."

He obeyed and gripped her wrist, removing her hand from his face. "You're playing a dangerous game."

"That's a start."

Catie placed her hand in his forearm. His pulse raced at her delicate caress.

"Seems you know what I'm after."

"Yeah. I know what you're after," he said, "and you're not gonna get it."

"Don't you think I'm pretty?" Catie curled her lips into a pout and entwined her arms around Chad's neck.

"Aw, damn." He pushed her away. "You have no idea what you're doing to me. This is really dangerous."

"It's what I want, Chad. What I've always wanted."

"Catie—"

"I never dated in high school. Did you know that? I've never even kissed a boy. I wanted you to be the first one to kiss my lips. Do it, Chad. Please." She closed her eyes.

He groaned. How easy it would be to lower his mouth to hers, to taste those succulent lips. He inhaled, and then unclamped her arms from around his neck.

"This isn't what you want," he said.

"I'm eighteen. I know damn well what I want, Chad. I know you want me, too. I can see it in your eyes. Your body language."

"You don't know the first thing about body language, Catie." He stomped across the gazebo, away from her, the loss of her body heat a deprivation he hadn't expected.

"I do. I feel that you want me."

"Fine." He gritted his teeth, clenched his fists. "You're not wrong. I want you. I want to rip your dress off and take you right here on the gazebo. And if Harper or your dad should walk by, to hell with them. I want to shove my tongue into your mouth, down your throat. I want to kiss your soft skin, your pretty nipples. I know they're pretty, Catie. I can see 'em through that damn dress you're wearing. I want to taste every inch of you. Kiss you between your legs until you can't see straight. I want to shove myself deep inside you. So deep you scream with the invasion."

Sweat trickled down his brow, tickling him. God, he wanted her. She stood before him, her cheeks glowing with redness, goose bumps on her bare arms.

"See? You're quivering. I scared you, didn't I? You're arousing a man's feeling in a grown man. And you're still a little girl. God, you have no idea what you're doing to me."

"No, Chad. You didn't scare me."

But he had. Her cracking voice gave her away.

"You're not ready for this. Not ready for me. Some day you'll thank me for not takin' what you think you're so ready to give." He banged one of his clenched fists against the railing of the gazebo. "Damn!"

Her hands curled into fists and she inched toward him. "I do know what I want, Chad. It's always been you. Always."

He held up his hand in a stop motion. "Don't come any closer, or I swear I won't be able to resist those cherry lips."

"That's okay." She smiled and closed her eyes, lifted her chin. "I'm legal now. You can have me. All of me."

Sweet temptation...but no, her body betrayed her words. She wanted him, but fear still gripped her.

He walked away while her eyes were still shut, and he didn't look back.

The white haze of sleep engulfed him. Catie came to him then, wearing a flight attendant outfit.

"May I fluff your pillow, sir?" she asked, smiling.

He longed to touch her pretty face. He extended his hand, but she smacked him away.

"No," she said. "Don't touch me. You did this to me. You. *You.*"

What? Tears streamed down her soft cheeks. He yearned to offer comfort, but she pushed him away again.

"Look at me. You did this. You did this."

Chad's eyes traveled down her body, to the juncture between her legs. Bright red blood stained her white capri pants.

The miscarriage.

"Baby, I'm sorry." His heart ached with despair as he reached for her.

But his hand touched only air. She was gone.

Chad awoke, sweat dribbling down his forehead.

Ms. Flirty approached. "Do you need anything, sir?"

"Yeah," he said. "I need to get to Paris."

"We'll be there in about three more hours, sir."

"Not soon enough," he grumbled and turned into his pillow.

No more sleep came. Only anguish. He loved Catie. More than anything. More than his own life. He loved her so much he thought it might hurt less to rip his heart right out of his chest than to live without her.

He'd been her first, and he'd give anything in the world, his entire fortune, to be her last.

★ ★ ★

"Oh, Dom, you are such a sight for sore eyes!" Catie ran into the Frenchman's arms.

"*Chérie*, we need to get you home," Dominic said. "You look like you have been run over by a train. *Mon Dieu*."

"I feel like I've been run over by a train. And a truck. And a herd of stampeding buffalo," Catie said. "I'm just glad to be here. It was a long flight."

"Not one you thought you'd be making so soon."

"Right." She sighed. Good old Dom. He'd take care of her.

Back at Dominic's Paris flat, Catie relaxed with a glass of Bordeaux and a crisp baguette.

"I've missed the wine," she said, "though the first thing I drank when I got to Colorado was a good old margarita."

"That lime monstrosity?"

"Yeah, and it was damn good." She closed her eyes, remembering that night. When Chad had danced with her, had kissed her on the dance floor. Was it possible only a little over a month had passed since then?

"*Chérie*, we need to get you to bed."

"I don't want to put you out."

"Do not be absurd. You need some rest. I can deal with the couch for one night. Tomorrow we will get you a futon."

"You don't have to."

"I know I don't have to. I want to. Now go take a shower." He picked up her small bag. "I'll put this in your room for you. It doesn't look like you brought much."

She sighed again. "I got out of town quickly."

"No matter. Tomorrow you can shop for whatever you need."

"Don't you have to work tomorrow?"

"I'm taking the day off."

"Not for me."

"Yes, for you. You're one of my dearest friends, Caitlyn. I'll be here for you."

Catie smiled. Dominic was such a savior. She could always count on him. If only she could count on her husband that same way.

She hadn't heard word one from him. Of course, her cell phone was dead. Still, if he cared...

Visions of their baby, now dead, tormented her. A little boy who looked like Chad. The image of his other baby, Linda's son, stole into her mind. Why had Chad abandoned his son?

She fell on the bed and closed her eyes. She'd shower in the morning.

★ ★ ★

"Rise and shine, lady of the manor!"

Catie opened her eyes to Dominic strolling about the room, opening the shades. Morning sunshine flowed into the room, hurting Catie's eyes.

"Goodness. What time is it?"

"Eight a.m., *chérie*."

"Oh, my." Catie sat up and stretched. Her body itched with grease and grime. She so needed a shower.

"Take care of yourself, *chérie*. I will have *café au lait* for you in the kitchen in half an hour."

"You're a gem, Dom."

Dominic's steam shower soothed her aching bones. She disconnected the showerhead and let the water pulse over her abdomen, relieving some of the residual cramping. She was still bleeding, and probably would for a few days, the doctor had said.

She dressed in some of Dom's sweats she found in the room. They hung on her, but they were soft and comfortable. She ambled out to the kitchen, sat down at the table, and fingered a flaky croissant.

"Here you go, just like you like it." Dominic set a cup of steaming *café au lait* in front of her. She inhaled the smoky aroma. *Mmmm.* She had missed this. She'd missed Dominic.

A knock interrupted her thoughts.

"That is Christian," Dominic said. "You sit tight."

"Caitlyn!" Christian pulled her up into a bear hug. "When Dom said you were returning, I was so happy."

She melted into the handsome blond's embrace. Oh, she had missed her friends. She inhaled the aroma of his jacket—stale cloves and smoke—Indonesian cigarettes. She'd never been able to convince either Dom or Chris to quit smoking. Right now, his scent was the sweetest thing she'd smelled in a long time. She inhaled again and closed her eyes.

Until a deep-timbre cut into her thoughts.

"Get your filthy French hands off my wife."

CHAPTER NINETEEN

Chad's possessive voice trickled over Catie like warm honey. She turned in Christian's arms and gazed into her husband's smoking dark eyes. They were sunken, a little wet.

Had he been worried?

"Chad. What are you doing here?"

"I came for my wife."

"But—"

"Get your hands off her." Chad stalked forward, his eyes glittering with rage. "I mean it, friend, or you'll wish you had."

"Chad, you don't understand."

"I understand plenty, sugar. You left me." He yanked her out of Christian's embrace. "How could you leave me? Without a word? I didn't know where you were, where you'd gone. You wouldn't answer your cell." He shook his head, his eyes boring into her. "Do you hate me that much?"

"I... I never hated you, Chad."

"She has been through a lot. Give her a break," Dominic said.

"When I want your opinion I'll ask for it," Chad said. "This is between my wife and me."

"But you don't understand—"

"I understand plenty. I come in here and I see one of you with your hands all over my wife. She's not yours, and she never will be. She's mine. Mine and mine alone. Let's go, Catie."

"Chad"—Catie broke away—"I'm not going with you."

"The hell you're not."

"You don't want me."

"I tracked you all the way across the world! For God's sake, of course I want you. I thought we had a deal."

"Chad, we never had any kind of deal. You and I...were not meant to be. You never wanted to be married. I never should have agreed to it. In fact, I'm not sure I did. I was in a haze about the pregnancy, and I just did whatever you told me. It was a mistake. A huge one. We'll get an annulment. Or worst case scenario, a divorce. I don't want anything from you."

The baby. She had to tell him the baby was gone. Then he'd understand. She turned to Christian and Dominic. "Would you guys excuse us? I need to talk to him. Alone."

"Of course," Dominic said, "but this is not a big flat."

"No," Catie said. "I meant we'll leave. Come on, Chad. Let's take a walk."

Despite the sunshine and the beauty of Paris, Catie's mood was gray. How could she tell him the baby was gone? He'd be so angry. Worse, he'd leave her.

"Have you ever been here before, Chad?" She stalled. "Is there anything you want to see? The Eiffel Tower? The Louvre?"

"Damn it, Catie, I didn't come here as a tourist. I came for you. Now tell me what the hell's going on."

She sighed. "Yeah. I owe you that much."

They reached a small café, and Catie took a seat at one of the outside tables. Chad sat next to her.

"*Café au lait, s'il vous plaît,*" she told the waiter, "*et deux croissants.*"

"What did you say?"

"I ordered coffee and croissants. Did you want something

else?"

"Bacon, eggs, and hash browns would be good. Maybe a Denver omelet."

"This is Paris, Chad, not Colorado. You'd be hard pressed to find that kind of breakfast here."

"I can't eat this fancy-schmancy food."

"That's okay. My guess is you won't be here long."

"What the hell is that supposed to mean?"

Catie's pulse quickened. She let out a breath. "It means... Well, I'll just come right out and say it." She cleared her throat and stared at her lap. "I lost the baby, Chad."

"I know."

Catie whipped her head up. "You know? Then why did you come here? I don't understand."

Chad took her hand. "I came here for you, Catie. I love you."

A tear trickled down Catie's cheek, warming her. He wanted her? "I don't understand."

He smiled. "What's not to understand? I've been an idiot, little bit. I love you. It just took me a while to figure it out. First, I thought you were too young. I couldn't get it out of my mind that I knew you when you were four and I was fifteen."

"Chad—"

"No. Let me finish. I'm so sorry I wasn't with you when you miscarried. I should have been. I should have been there through all of this. I should have treated you like the wife you deserve to be, instead of a call girl available only for my pleasure. Can you ever forgive me?"

Catie fought the warmth that threatened to glow within her. Chad had a lot to answer for.

"I want to forgive you. I truly do." More tears threatened

to fall, but she held them back. "But there's so much I need to understand. I went to see Linda."

"I know."

"You should have told me, Chad."

"There's nothing to tell."

Had she heard right? "Uh, having a child by another woman is definitely something your wife should know."

Chad's dark eyes widened. "What? You mean Linda didn't tell you?"

"Tell me what? We met briefly. She seemed like a perfectly nice person. I met Jack. He's a beautiful little boy, though he doesn't look anything like you."

"There's a good reason for that."

"Which would be?"

"He's not mine, Catie."

"What? I saw the DNA results in your file."

"So you did a little snooping?"

"Yes. Yes, I did. But only after I got a phone call from Linda, and I intercepted some IMs on your computer."

"I'm sure sorry about that, sugar. I wish you'd have come to me."

"How could I? You were treating me like a common whore. You ignored me during the day, screwed me during the night. I should have..."

"You should have what?"

"I should have turned you away at night. I wanted to. I just couldn't."

"Because you wanted me as much as I wanted you."

"I've always wanted you, Chad. I don't seem to have any control where you're concerned. Yes, it started as puppy love, but it never went away." She sighed. "Four years in France, and it still didn't go away."

"Aw, sugar."

"Don't start sweet-talkin' me. You still have a lot of explaining to do about Linda."

"Frankly, sugar, I'm a little insulted."

"Why on earth should *you* be insulted?"

"Because, if Jack were truly my child, do you really think I'd let him live in that little cow town with Linda and her crazy parents? Don't you think I'd have him on the ranch with me, giving him the best of everything? Everything my pa gave me? God, sugar."

"Crazy parents? I don't know anything about that. And I didn't think about...the other stuff."

"No, you didn't really think, did you?"

"Can you blame me?"

"No," he said sheepishly, "I can't."

"Now, the truth about Linda and Jack, please."

"Well, I want to know why you didn't just ask me about it?"

"Because you hardly spoke to me, Chad. And I wasn't sure how you'd take it if you knew I'd been...lurking around your office trying to figure out...oh, you know. Of course I couldn't ask you."

"You could have asked Annie. You and she are close, and she knows the truth."

"No, Chad, I couldn't ask her. It was too hard to talk about. Plus, she had assured me you'd had women come around claiming you fathered their children before and that you'd had them checked out. I assumed she didn't know about Jack." She touched his forearm, offering an olive branch. "Would *you* please tell me?"

He took her hand from his arm and covered it with his own. "Linda Rhine is a woman I had a...well, I'm not proud of this, but you no doubt know how I was when I was younger."

Catie scoffed. "When you were younger?"

"Yeah, okay. She was a one-night stand. Five or so years ago, during the stock show in Denver. That's the time Dusty and Zach hooked up. She was a friend of this champion barrel racer, Sydney something or other, who hooked up with Dusty's brother, Sam. After dinner, we ended up back at my hotel room."

"And?"

"And nothing. We had sex. I used a condom. I have always used a condom. But as you and I proved, condoms aren't always foolproof."

Catie shook her head. "No, they're not."

"So anyway, about a year ago, right after Ma died, Linda shows up at my doorstep, holding little Jack's hand. Tells me he's mine. That she can prove it.

"I say go for it. The kid doesn't look anything like me. You know that. I go into Denver for a blood test, and she shows up three days later with the papers.

"Well, it don't take a genius to realize it's forged. My PI, Larry—he's the one who tracked you down, by the way—got the whole thing figured out in no time flat. Linda's mother is a con artist and has been milking money out of unsuspecting people for years. She arranged for a shady doctor to perform the tests and fix the result. Once Larry uncovered that scam, I got a court order for another test, and of course this one came up negative."

"But the document said you were the father."

"You saw the first blood test. The forged one. The rest of

the papers are in a different file, under Linda's mother's name, Dorothy Smith."

"Oh." Catie's cheeks warmed. She'd jumped to a very wrong conclusion, though anyone else would have thought the same. She faced Chad. "If he's not yours, why did Linda call you?"

"Yeah, that's a fair question." Chad took a bite of his croissant and a gulp of coffee. "Linda didn't want to con me. It was her mother's idea. But Linda was desperate, and she knew I had money. Little Jack, see, has a rare blood disorder called aplastic anemia. Linda needed money bad. She broke down crying when I called her on the phony test. Told me she'd never wanted to do it. Her mother had basically convinced her it was her only choice."

"What about Jack?"

"I'm gettin' to that. You see, little Jack was innocent in all this. He wasn't mine, but I'd grown kind of fond of the little tyke. He's right about the same age as Sean. It'd been a while since I'd done anything nice for anyone, and I thought about my ma. About how forgiving she always was, and very giving of her time and money to charitable causes. What would she have wanted me to do? So I decided to fund Jack's treatment."

Catie's hand flew to her mouth. "Oh, Chad."

"But if you're against it, we'll stop. This is *our* decision now, not mine alone."

She squeezed his hand. "I'd never ask you to take something away from a child. Never. He needs you. How is he doing?"

"He's well, thank goodness. It doesn't cost so much now. It's just checkups, to make sure he's still okay. It cost quite a bit for the bone marrow donation and transplant last year. I send her a small amount each month for incidentals, and Linda calls me or IMs me when she needs something else."

Catie smiled. She hadn't known she could love this man more than she already did. "It's a wonderful thing you're doing for Linda and Jack."

Jack chuckled. "I'm trying to imagine the surprise on Linda's face when she found out I was married. No doubt she figured no one would ever rope me in."

"Yeah, well, you didn't exactly want to be roped. It was an accident." She signed and touched her belly. "An accident that's now moot."

He touched her cheek. "I don't want you to think of it that way. Yeah, the condom broke, but that wasn't your fault or mine."

She sniffed. "You tried to make it my fault."

"I was a fool. I'm sorry. Can you forgive me?"

"I don't know, Chad. Are there any more secrets? Anything more I need to know about? I know you haven't lived like monk."

"No, I haven't, but I'm willing to from now on."

"What?"

"I mean, I'm willing to live in a sexually exclusive relationship. With you. My wife. My only love."

"Oh, Chad. Do you really love me?"

"With all my heart."

Sunshine spread through Catie's body, and she broke into tears.

"Now come on. Don't cry, sugar. I'm liable to think you don't love me back."

"Oh, I love you back, Chad McCray. I've loved you for seventeen years."

He leaned forward and took her mouth in a searing kiss. When their waiter came by with more croissants and cleared his throat, Catie's cheeks warmed.

"So are you ever going to tell me your secret, little bit?"

"Little bit? Please, Chad."

He laughed. "Okay, sugar. Now, about your secret."

"I have no idea what you're referring to. I don't have any secrets."

"That first night, at the Bullfrog, you said there was a reason you stayed away for four years. You said you'd tell me sometime. Now, sugar, a wife shouldn't have any secrets from her husband."

Catie shook her head. "You haven't figured that out yet?" She ruffled his hair. "You *are* dense."

"Was it because of me, sugar? Because of...that night in the gazebo?"

She sighed. "Yeah, well, that night, and the previous ten years, I thought if I stayed away I'd get over you."

"Damn, you have no idea how much I wanted you that night."

"Yeah, I do. I know. Because I wanted you that much."

"I'm not sure you get it, Catie. You were still a baby to me, and there I was, having these feelings. Lusty feelings. I wanted to take you right there, and I didn't much care if your daddy walked by. It felt all wrong to want you that way, but at the same time, it felt very, very right."

Catie's mouth dropped open. "Really?"

"I had no idea you were my destiny, sugar. No idea at all. I always knew you were a pretty thing, but that night, things changed. It...scared me."

Catie smiled. "The womanizing Chad McCray? Scared

of a little eighteen-year-old girl?"

"You brought me to my knees that night, sugar. If you hadn't left the next day, I would have come back for you."

"Yeah?"

"Yeah. But you did. And I thought that was your way of telling me you'd changed your mind. Part of me was angry. I hadn't been able to sleep at all that night. But part of me was relieved. I was scared to death we'd do something you'd later regret. I thought it was better with you gone. We'd both be out of temptation's way."

"You felt the same way when you saw me again when I returned, didn't you?"

"Yeah, I was still afraid we'd do something you'd regret. But I couldn't help myself. I wanted you so badly, more than I ever wanted another woman. I was afraid you'd get hurt. You know me. I didn't think I could commit." He chuckled, shaking his head, playing with her fingers. "Who knew I'd fall madly in love with you?"

Catie sighed. "Those have got to be the sweetest words I've ever heard."

"Well, sugar, you're going to be hearing them a lot. Because I'm never going to get tired of saying them." He took both her hands in his. "I love you, Catie Bay McCray. Now and always. I'm going to spend the rest of my life making you and our children happy. You won't regret marrying me. I promise you."

"Oh, Chad."

"And no more secrets between us. We tell each other everything, okay?"

"Okay."

"I just thought of the perfect wedding gift for you, too."

"What?"

"One of those things old ladies wear around their necks to call for help, for when you fall all over your clumsy ass." His eyes glittered with amusement.

She broke into laughter. "I think I'll be okay. Heck, if I can walk down that runway in a green bikini, I can do anything now."

"Something else, sugar. From now on, you wear that green bikini only for me."

"Chad, it wasn't near as revealing as what Amber and some of the others wore."

"Maybe not. But you're my woman. My wife. And those jewels of yours are for my eyes only now."

"Okay." Her cheeks warmed.

"You can tell those frisky Frenchmen to keep their paws off you, too. Like I told you that day in the stable, you're mine and you always will be."

"Frisky Frenchmen?"

"Yeah, that blond pretty boy had you in a tight clinch when I showed up. I nearly punched his lights out."

Catie laughed. "Christian? And Dominic? Oh, Chad, that's too funny."

"Nothing funny about it from where I'm standing. They can leave you well enough alone. Were either of them ever... more than friends, Catie? Did they insist that you come back here?"

"They are wonderful friends, and they'd do anything in the world for me, but I swear to you, it's nothing more than that." She burst into giggles again.

"What's so damn funny?"

"It's just that...there could never be anything between me

and either Christian or Dominic."

"Why not? You're beautiful. The most beautiful woman in the world."

"They might actually agree with you, but it wouldn't matter." She tightened her grip on his hand. "They're lovers, Chad. They're gay."

CHAPTER TWENTY

"You guys are too much," Catie said. "You don't have to do this, especially since I'm already married."

"And miss the chance to put together a wedding for our good friend?" Dominic toyed with Catie's veil. "We'd never forgive you. We live for this kind of thing."

"I've always wanted to get married in Notre Dame Cathedral," Catie said. "Too bad the wait list is a mile long."

"My little chapel will be perfect, *chérie*." He touched up her lipstick. "They're very accommodating and not prejudiced at all. Chris and I are having our commitment ceremony there."

"Chad and I will be back for that in a couple months, I promise." She pressed her lips together and Dominic blotted them on a hanky. "How is he doing, by the way?"

"Chris is attending to your cowboy, now."

Catie laughed. "I bet Chad is seriously uncomfortable with that."

"Probably." Dominic joined in the laughter. "But no one knows men's fashion like Chris. Your *homme* will look *magnifique*. I have to tell you, Caitlyn, he is scrumptious."

"That he is." She slapped Dom's hand playfully. "And he's all mine."

"Don't worry about me. I'm mad about Chris. I've never gone for the Alpha cowboy type." He sighed. "They are nice to look at, though."

"They certainly, are," Catie agreed.

Dominic grasped Catie's shoulders, and his gaze met hers. "Tell me, Caitlyn, that this is what you want. This man."

She nodded. "He's what I want, Dom. He's all I've ever wanted. Since I was a little kid. And now he wants me, too." She rubbed her tummy, a sway of sadness waving over her. "I wish I hadn't lost our baby. But we'll have more. A whole slew of 'em, Chad says." She smiled. "My mama had several miscarriages between Harper and me. That's why there's such a difference in our ages."

"It is common, *chérie*. Come," he said, taking her hand and placing it in the crook of his arm. "It is time to walk you down the aisle."

★ ★ ★

She was a vision. A goddess. Chad's pulse raced as Catie drifted toward him, veiled in gossamer cream. She clutched Dominic's arm tightly. Next to him stood Christian, blond and dressed to the nines, as though he'd stepped out of a men's fashion magazine.

Catie flashed a radiant smile as Dominic handed her off to him. Chad leaned down and kissed her cheek, inhaling her fresh, clean aroma. Raspberries. God, how he'd missed her.

No wedding night tonight. She had to heal from the miscarriage. How would he cope? He smiled to himself. He'd cope. He'd wait. His gorgeous Caitlyn Bay McCray, whom he loved more than life itself with a passion he never knew existed, was well worth it.

Besides, she'd promised to take care of him. His tuxedo trousers tightened as he imagined those ruby lips touching all his intimate places.

He should wait for her. A gentleman would. A gentleman would hold her and let her know she meant the world to him, and that he'd wait to make love until she could be a full participant.

Course as he'd told her on many an occasion, he was no gentleman.

CONTINUE THE TEMPTATION SAGA WITH
BOOK FOUR

Taming ANGELINA

Available Now

Keep reading for an excerpt!

CHAPTER ONE

Long black lashes fringed eyes like perfect emeralds. Cheeks shimmered the color of the palest pink rose. Dark hair hung in two ponytails on either side of an oval face. The red-and-white gingham blouse tied below round breasts—with just a touch of cleavage showing—screamed country girl. The Daisy Dukes, long shapely legs, and fire-engine red toenails peeking out from strappy leather flip-flops screamed siren.

Tall, too. He loved tall women. At six-three, he liked his women to fit his frame.

His groin tightened. He'd never been immune to a pretty woman, and she was about as gorgeous as he'd seen—the perfect combination of innocence and heat, sparkle and sultry, virtue and corruption. How would those cherry lips feels against his own? Against...other places?

The two ponytails that would be ridiculous on most women worked on her. Dark curls tumbled over each shoulder. He imagined her sans blouse, sans hair ribbons, that silky hair cascading over peachy-pink shoulders, rosy-tipped breasts.

How it might feel between his fingers, brushing his chest...

Good lord, she is beautiful.

Then she spoke.

"Hand, I'm looking for Rafe Grayhawk."

Hand? Not so beautiful inside. The derision in her tone was unmistakable. He fought the urge to ignore her. He was an employee here at McCray Landing. If this woman was looking for him, she probably had a reason.

"I'm Rafe Grayhawk."

She whipped her hands to her round hips. "I hear you can teach me to ride."

Huh? Who is this woman anyway? She vaguely resembled his boss's wife, though Catie was more refreshing, less "nose-stuck-in-the-air."

"I can teach anyone to ride, honey." He eyed her up and down. "But not in that getup. Who are you, anyway?"

"Angelina Bay. Catie's sister. And don't call me honey."

Rafe held out his hand. "Nice to meet you."

She didn't return the gesture. He dropped his hand back to his side.

"I used to ride a little. I was rodeo queen quite a while ago. But I didn't keep up with it. My daddy says if I'm going to own one of his ranches someday it's high time I learned to ride decently. We don't have any hands at our ranch who have the time or talent to teach me, in his opinion. Daddy wants the best. According to Chad McCray, you're it."

"Why not ask your sister? She's as good a rider as anyone."

"Clearly you haven't heard the good news." Angelina scuffed one sandaled foot in the dirt of the stall. "She's expecting, and since she had a miscarriage the first time, she and Chad are being ridiculously overprotective this time."

Didn't sound unreasonable to Rafe. His mother had struggled with miscarriages and his father had been very protective, but Angelina's voice registered indignation over her sister's decision to put her pregnancy first.

Teach this piece of work to ride? Not in this lifetime.

He turned back to the horse he was currying. "I'm afraid I can't help you. McCray expects all his hands to put in forty hours a week here."

"I already okayed it through him. Didn't I just say he said you're the best to teach me? Sheesh."

Eye roll. He wasn't looking at her, but he knew her pupils were curving upward against her lids.

"Darlin', you've got a sight to learn about askin' for a favor."

"I'm not asking for a favor, hand. You'll be well paid."

Hand again? Christ, I have a name. He turned and gazed into those eyes clear as the Mediterranean Sea. "Well paid, huh? Just how much constitutes 'well paid' to you?"

"Fifty dollars an hour."

A fair price, for sure. Not worth it to put up with this prima donna, though.

"Make it a hundred."

The porcelain hands dashed to her hips again.

"A hundred? Are you kidding me? Fifty is the going rate around here."

"Then I'm sure you won't have any problem finding someone else at that price. Nice meeting you." He turned his back to her.

"But Chad says you're the best."

"The man speaks the truth." Rafe smoothed the gelding's dark mane.

"Seventy-five is as high as I'll go."

Rafe pursed his lips. Seventy-five dollars an hour would go a long way helping his father get out of that damned trailer park. For the last couple of years, Rafe and his brother, Tom, had been putting all their extra money toward a place in Arizona for Jack Grayhawk. Since the death of Rafe's mother, his dad had been wasting away in that old dump. Though only fifty, he'd had to leave construction work after a debilitating injury to his hip. He could still get around, but work was out of the question. He drew a small disability pension, but it wasn't enough. He also suffered from chronic asthma, and though Colorado weather wasn't bad, the dryer Arizona weather and mild winters would be better. Yeah, this money would sure help. Rafe turned around and gazed at the slender woman. Spending time looking at Angelina Bay would be no hardship. Still, to put up with her attitude...

"The price is a hundred. Take it or leave it."

"I'll leave it."

The beauty turned on her heels and marched toward the door of the barn.

Shit, I should have taken the seventy-five.

He could have made life easier for his dad. Jack could take Lilia, the Mexican woman who'd kept house for him for the last five years, with him. Since Finola Grayhawk had passed on three years ago, Lilia cooked and cleaned in exchange for room and board in Rafe and Tom's old room. Lilia had reduced her hours as a receptionist to part time to help keep house for Jack. The two would have had a wonderful new life in Arizona.

Ah well, Rafe had no doubt saved himself a lifetime's worth of headache. He put the currycomb down and grabbed the stiff bristle brush. This particular gelding, Adonis, loved the stiff bristle brush. Rafe started at the neck with short flicking motions. "That's a good boy."

A throat cleared behind him. He turned. Angelina.

"You still here? Thought you'd marched out in a huff."

"A hundred it is then, hand."

"There ain't enough money in the world for me to put up with you calling me 'hand.'"

"That's what I call all the hands."

"They have names, you know."

"You expect me to remember all those names?"

"Why not? They remember yours, don't they?"

"That's different. I'm the boss's daughter, and there's only one of me."

Thank God. If another Angelina existed, he'd lose all hope for the world. "You're not the boss's daughter here."

"I'm the boss's sister-in-law."

"Whatever. You want my help? The price is a hundred an hour, and if you call me 'hand' one more time, all deals are off."

"Fine. Rafe, then."

"How about Mr. Grayhawk?"

"You can't be serious."

"Oh, I am, Miss Bay." *Let's see how she handles this one.*

"Of course you should call me Miss Bay. I'm the boss and you're the help."

Help? Seriously? Normally he'd think twice about getting into it with his boss's sister-in-law, but Chad McCray respected him and his work, and this little snot brought out the worst in him. "I obviously have something you want. I won't deal with disrespect from anyone, especially not a flouncy ranch girl."

Hands to hips again. Did she have two indentations there? "Girl? I happen to be thirty-two years old."

Thirty-two? He'd have guessed her younger than his own age of twenty-five. The years had been kind to Miss Bay. She had the skin and body of a nineteen-year-old. She was a beauty. On the outside, at least.

"Thirty-two years old and acting like a spoiled brat? Grow up, Angelina."

"Miss Bay."

"Angelina. And you'll call me Rafe. I hate Mr. Grayhawk."

She tapped her foot on the barn floor. "It was your idea."

"I was trying to make a point. You were being disrespectful."

"I'm not used to being respectful to hands."

"Well, get used to it. We're people, just like you, and disrespect hurts us, just like it hurts you." Though he doubted she'd ever experienced disrespect.

Her eyes widened—just a little, but he'd made her think. For a second, anyway.

"All right...*Rafe.* When can we start?"

"You got a horse?"

"Yes. Just bought her. A beautiful black mare named Belle."

"Have her brought over by seven tonight."

"Okay."

"And I'll see you tomorrow. Six a.m. sharp."

This time when her hands flew to her hips her eyes turned to saucers. "Six a.m.? Sorry. I don't do the crack of dawn."

Rafe shook his head. "And you expect to own your father's ranch someday? Do you have any idea what time he gets up? Chad and Catie are up before five every morning."

"I'm not Catie."

She was right about that. Did the two of them really come from the same gene pool? The physical evidence was there, but little else.

"Six a.m.," he said, "and wear clothes suitable for riding."

She stormed out, sulking.

Rafe chuckled. No way would she show up.

* * *

"Angie, how are you?" Debra Montgomery took her arm. "What can we show you today?"

"Whatever you have that's new."

Deb nodded. "I'll call in the reserves."

Angie was known around town for her shopping sprees. She ignored the snotty remarks that she alone kept Deb's Boutique in business. Right now she wanted new clothes, and then she'd head over to the beauty shop for some pampering.

Because she felt like it, that's why.

"We just got in some great new studded jeans from New York," Deb said. "I'll have Lori bring some out in your size."

Angie tried on six pairs of jeans, discarded three, and added the other three to her pile. "I'll need some shirts to go with these," she told Lori, the red-haired clerk she hadn't seen before.

Lori brought in shirt after shirt, but none suited Angie. She piled them back into Lori's arms. "Don't you have anything that doesn't look like it came from a discount store tent sale? Sheesh!"

Lori sighed. "I'll check with Deb."

Deb herself came over. "I'm sorry our selection of blouses isn't to your liking today, Angie. You know I stock only the latest fashions."

Angie rolled her eyes. "Do you have anything else?"

"Lori's getting a few more for you."

"Maybe you should light a fire under her. Your new clerk is incredibly slow."

Deb smiled. Deb always smiled. She had to. Angie spent a lot of money in her boutique.

Lori came out with four more blouses. Angie touched the

fabric. "Is this supposed to be silk?"

"That one's rayon," Lori said.

"Rayon? A man-made fabric?"

"Rayon is a semi-synthetic, actually," Deb said. "All the top houses in New York and Europe use it. You know that."

"Whatever." Angie took the blouses. "I'll try them on." She walked back into the dressing room.

"How do you stand her?" she heard Lori whisper.

Angie shook her head as her temper rose. "You may want to tell your new clerk to install soundproof doors on your dressing rooms. I heard that!"

"I'm sorry, Angie," Deb's voice said. "I'll take care of you myself today."

Angie discarded three of the blouses into Deb's waiting arms. "You should fire that new girl. Hasn't she ever heard that the customer is always right?"

"Lori knows fashion," Deb said. "I'm sorry she insulted you, but I won't fire her. She came highly recommended, and just in the week she's been here she's made more sales than Gwen did all month."

"Fine," Angie said. "Put the clothes on my tab and have them delivered. And don't expect to see me in here again as long as that little snot is working here."

She walked out the door and headed to Judy's Beauty Shop across the street.

"Amber, are you free?"

The pretty platinum blond manicurist, Bakersville's reigning rodeo queen, looked up. "Hi, Angie. Yeah, I can squeeze you in. Manicure?"

"Mani and pedi. It's been a day."

Amber motioned her over to her table. "What's going on?

Deb didn't have what you were looking for?"

Angie noted the sarcasm in Amber's voice but decided to ignore it. She had bigger fish to fry. "Deb never has what I'm looking for, but that's not the main problem." She sighed. "My father thinks I need riding lessons."

Amber picked up her cuticle nippers. "I thought you knew how to ride."

"I do. Sort of. I just haven't done it in a while. I was good enough to do the rodeo queen patterns a million years ago, but I was just never that into it. I'm not Catie."

"Catie's a natural."

"Totally. Did you hear she's pregnant again?"

"Yeah, she stopped in yesterday and told me. I'm so happy for her and Chad."

"Yeah, me too." At least she wanted to be. But Catie's pregnancy only reminded her of her own biological clock. Her baby sister would be a mother before she would. Not that she had any grand desire to be a mother. At least that's what she kept telling herself.

Hell, how did I get on this subject?

"Can we get back to my riding?"

"Sure. You brought up Catie being pregnant."

Oh yeah. "I know. But right now this riding thing is driving me nuts."

"Riding is tough to learn, for sure, but there's nothing like it. I love it myself."

"Maybe you could teach me then."

Amber laughed. "Me? Are you kidding? I can get around, but I'm not qualified to instruct anyone."

Crap. Oh well. She'd approached a few local riding instructors before Chad led her to Rafe Grayhawk. They'd all turned her down flat. Course she hadn't offered any of them a hundred bucks an hour, but they'd all seemed eager to tell her how they were too busy to teach the older Bay daughter how to ride a horse properly. Was she that difficult?

"Do I have a...reputation in this town?" she asked Amber.

Amber's gaze was locked on Angie's cuticles. Was she deliberately avoiding eye contact?

"I'm not sure what you mean."

"I mean...as being...difficult to work with, or something?"

Amber cleared her throat. "You're not difficult with me. We get along great."

"I know. I guess I mean... Oh heck, I don't know what I mean."

Amber placed Angie's right hand into the little bowl of solution and grabbed her other. This time she didn't look away. "Do you want me to be honest with you?"

"Of course."

"You're a friend to me as well as a client, so I don't want this to hurt our relationship."

"It won't. I promise."

"Okay." Amber sighed. "People who get to know you generally like you. That's not the problem."

"What is, then?"

"Well, you don't get to know a lot of people, for one thing. There are people you feel are..."

"Are what? What are you trying to say, Amber?"

"Let's put it this way. Would we be friends if I weren't friends with your sister? Would you have bothered getting to know me?"

"Of course. You're the best manicurist Judy's ever hired."

"That's not what I mean."

"What do you mean then?"

Amber sighed. "Sure, you'd let me do your nails. That's one thing. But would we hang out together during happy hour at The Bullfrog? Would we spend the day in Denver shopping?"

Angie bit her lip. Amber had a point. She'd never made friends with her manicurist before.

"And there's another thing."

God. "What?"

"No one wants to work for you."

"What do you mean? You work for me."

"I do your nails. Judy does your hair. We don't teach you to ride."

"I don't see what the difference is."

"We pamper you." Amber let out a giggle. "You're very good at being pampered. You won't get any pampering learning to ride. Riding is hard work. Don't get me wrong. I love it. The rewards are great. But you will not be pampered."

Angie's hackles rose. Who did Amber think she was? "It sounds like you're saying I'm spoiled."

Amber concentrated on the cuticles again. "You asked me to be honest, and you said it wouldn't harm our relationship."

"So you're admitting it? You think I'm spoiled?"

"I think you're a great person. I like you. We're friends, remember?"

"So I'm not spoiled?"

Amber started filing, still averting her gaze. "Let's put it this way. Remember a couple months ago when Judy added a touch too much red to your hair color?"

Angie remembered well. She'd looked like Elmo. "Yeah, I vaguely recall it."

"You called her incompetent and threatened to put her out of business. Never mind that she fixed your hair that same day, free of charge."

Warmth flooded to Angie's cheeks. *Yes, I overreacted.* "I apologized for that."

"I know you did, and Judy's still happy to have your business."

"She's the best hairdresser in this town."

"That she is. You knew it then, too."

Angie stiffened in her chair. "But demanding excellence doesn't mean I'm spoiled."

"No, it doesn't," Amber agreed. "But throwing a fit when you don't get it does."

Did I really throw a fit? She sighed. *Yeah, I did. Poor Judy. It's a wonder she still lets me back in her shop.*

Determination gripped her. The town of Bakersville would see a new Angelina Bay. She'd learn to ride as well as Catie, and she'd do it without throwing a single tantrum.

Well, she'd try, anyway.

"Do you know a ranch hand at Catie's named Rafe Grayhawk?"

Amber smiled. "Yeah, I've met him a few times. He's a hottie."

Hottie? That term didn't do Rafe Grayhawk justice. Angie hadn't been able to take her eyes off the tall, broad-shouldered man. The streams of sunlight through the boards on the barn ceiling had cast little highlights of indigo onto his long black hair. He'd worn a checkered shirt rolled up at the sleeves, and those forearms as they curried the horse...so sexy. His jeans clung just loosely enough over what she knew must be a fantastic butt. Yeah, she was a butt girl.

Give me a nice tight ass over pecs any day.

Though she didn't mind pecs. What might Rafe look like

without his shirt?

She imagined he smelled like the musky outdoors. Course, she hadn't been able to smell anything but horse this morning.

She shook her head to clear it. Gorgeous as he was, he'd been a jerk. Who did he think he was? *I am his employer's sister, for God's sake.*

"He's going to teach me to ride."

"Wow, really? He gives lessons?" Amber smiled as she massaged Angie's right forearm. "Come to think of it, I'm getting a little rusty. Could use a refresher course."

Something sharp cut into Angie's gut. A twinge of...what? Jealousy? Not possible. She had no interest in Rafe Grayhawk. He was way beneath her. So why did it bother her that Amber indicated an interest in him? Of course Amber was interested. She was female, she was straight, and she had a pulse. Who wouldn't be attracted to Rafe Grayhawk?

"You don't need a refresher course, rodeo queen. You ride great."

"Still, to spend some time in the company of that hunk—"

"He charges a hundred dollars an hour." That ought to get her.

"A hundred an hour? He must be damn good."

He'd better be.

She'd find out in the morning.

Early in the morning.

MESSAGE FROM HELEN HARDT

Dear Reader,

Thank you for reading *Taking Catie*. If you want to find out about my current backlist and future releases, please like my Facebook page: **www.facebook.com/HelenHardt** and join my mailing list: **www.helenhardt.com/signup/**. I often do giveaways. If you're a fan and would like to join my street team to help spread the word about my books, you can do so here: **www.facebook.com/groups/hardtandsoul/**. I regularly do awesome giveaways for my street team members.

If you enjoyed the story, please take the time to leave a review on a site like Amazon or Goodreads. I welcome all feedback.

I wish you all the best!

Helen

ALSO BY HELEN HARDT

The Sex and the Season Series:
Lily and the Duke
Rose in Bloom
Lady Alexandra's Lover
Sophie's Voice
The Perils of Patricia (Coming Soon)

The Temptation Saga:
Tempting Dusty
Teasing Annie
Taking Catie
Taming Angelina
Treasuring Amber
Trusting Sydney
Tantalizing Maria

The Steel Brothers Saga:
Craving
Obsession
Possession
Melt (Coming December 20th, 2016)
Burn (Coming February 14th, 2017)
Surrender (Coming May 16th, 2017)

Daughters of the Prairie:
The Outlaw's Angel
Lessons of the Heart
Song of the Raven

ACKNOWLEDGMENTS

Taking Catie is a puppy love turned true love story and marks the last of the hunky McCray brothers. But don't worry, Bakersville is home to many more gorgeous men!

So many people helped along the way in bringing this book to you. Celina Summers, Michele Hamner Moore, Jenny Rarden, Coreen Montagna, Kelly Shorten, David Grishman, Meredith Wild, Jonathan Mac, Kurt Vachon, Yvonne Ellis— thank you all for your expertise and guidance. Eternal thanks to Waterhouse Press for the expert rebranding of the series.

And thanks most of all to you, the readers. Up next is Catie's older sister, Angie, who meets her match in a hot ranch hand in *Taming Angelina*. Don't miss the thrilling fourth installment in the *Temptation Saga*!

ABOUT THE AUTHOR

New York Times and *USA Today* Bestselling author Helen Hardt's passion for the written word began with the books her mother read to her at bedtime. She wrote her first story at age six and hasn't stopped since. In addition to being an award winning author of contemporary and historical romance and erotica, she's a mother, a black belt in Taekwondo, a grammar geek, an appreciator of fine red wine, and a lover of Ben and Jerry's ice cream. She writes from her home in Colorado, where she lives with her family. Helen loves to hear from readers.

Visit her here:
www.facebook.com/HelenHardt

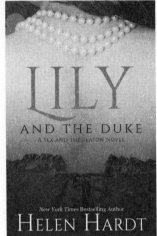